--Kim N., owner, Lady of America fitness club & Spa Lady
(Parma, Ohio)

WHAT PEOPLE ARE SAYING . . .

"In TRANSITIONS (Short Stories For A Rainy Day) author Cathy Jo has given us literary snippets into lives that seemed either ripped from the headlines or from experiences of our friends---or maybe even ourselves. The stories portray situations that are true to life and give you a taste of the talent that put them together. Whether it is discussing something serious like relationships, sexual assault and issues dealing with various forms of abuse and neglect, TRANSITIONS helps up to see that all things may have a season but they don't have to define who we are as individuals. I'm curious to see how much of the book reflects issues that the author herself has had to deal with, however, one of the great things about fiction is that you are able to discuss parts of your healing and situations in a way that can entertain as well as get others to think, and maybe even provide a little bit of healing along the way. From beginning to end Cathy Jo's TRANSITIONS delivers a literary buffet sure to be enjoyed."
--C.A. Webb "Conversations Book Club" (Jackson, MS)

"What I appreciated most about Cathy Jo's writing is the realism portrayed in the characters and their situations. In Reflections-In Memoriam, the character didn't allow her past to negatively influence her future and so she chose to help others with similar backgrounds to cope and ultimately make choices they could live with peacefully. Not every situation has a happy ending but I think we can learn something from each encounter. It's up to us to decide how we allow it to affect us."
--DKG (Cleveland, Ohio)

"....The stories in this collection focus primarily on the complicated lives of African-American women, but the plots move in a variety of ways and take some surprising turns that can be shocking, often tragic, and always candid. In each of these stories, Cathy Jo paints an expressive picture of these characters lives that seem to reach out to connect with us and challenge us in ways we might not expect, giving her readers something to think about beyond the basic entertainment value of the story."

--JD (Cleveland, Ohio)

"Cathy Jo's "Transitions" exceeded my expectations! I love her style. Her short stories are obviously of human interest and each carry a strong message. Some of the humor made me laugh out loud! Her characters literally came to life! I was impressed with her intricate knowledge and language of each character, male and female, and their respective professions! Each of the stories left me wanting more. I can't wait for her next production! Great job Cathy Jo!"

--Gretha Kelson, Writer of Short Stories, Novels, Songs, Poetry

"What spectacular short stories. Thanks Cathy Jo for making the characters come alive in every story. I really enjoy reading this book — I couldn't put it down. Keep up the good work."

--Karima

"Transitions is truly a book that should be read on one of those days that you are feeling down and you need a pick me up, or its raining outside and you just want to curl up on the couch with a good book. A book everyone should read, delivers on all counts, it will put you in the lives of the characters mentioned in the different stories."

--Nadine

"I absolutely love how fluid you write...the stories just absolutely flow. And each story is kept interesting. I can feel the emotions while reading... and in my head, I can imagine the storyline being played out....like a movie :)"

TRANSITIONS

TRANSITIONS

SHORT STORIES FOR A RAINY DAY

CATHY JO

Published by
Twisted Word Publishing
http://www.twistedwordpublishing.com
P. O. Box 46165
Bedford, Ohio 44146

Cover Design by Carol Drummond
http://www.drummondesign.com
Twisted Word logo design by Kevin Drummond

ISBN 978-0-9834259-3-9

Revised ed.

This is a work of fiction. Names, characters, places and incidents either are the product of the author's imagination or are used fictitiously, and any resemblance to actual persons, living or dead, events, or locales is entirely coincidental.

Printed in the United States of America

*This book is dedicated to all those who have a writer living inside
of them but who are too afraid to unleash it.*

CONTENTS

ACKNOWLEDGEMENTS

Thank you first to all of my family members who were supportive of me during the writing of this book. Special thanks to my sisters Linda and Diane Keeley. To my baby brother (smile), Wayne, who took care of my yard work so I could finally finish what I'd started, thank you!

Thank you to my editors, Susan Petrone and Wendy Wetzel, for not being afraid to tell me the truth.

Thank you to the Page Turners writing group.

To my coworkers (you know who you are) who gave me valuable feedback way back when, when I first entertained the idea of becoming a published writer, thank you.

A big thank you to all the staff at the Cleveland Public Library and the Cuyahoga County Public Library systems who were there in the wee hours of the morning to answer my questions via KnowItNow.

Finally, thank you to all those who allowed me to go on and on about my stories. Without your smiles of encouragement and listening ears, I don't know that I would have had the courage to take such a big leap.

A NOTE FROM THE AUTHOR

Thank you for purchasing my book. While the events that take place in the stories are purely fictitious, keep in mind that although they may not be my truth or yours, someone has or might be experiencing an identical situation to any one of the characters in this book. So there really can be no true originality in fiction. What differentiates one novel, or story, from another is really in the way the author conveys it.

In reading fiction, remember that the meaning you take away from the story may not necessarily be what someone else may take away, even if the ending may seem obvious to you. Fiction, like poetry, can be highly subjective. That said, the stories in this collection are designed to make you think, reflect. With every choice we make there is a consequence—positive or negative.

Some stories in this collection may not be to your personal liking, and others may touch a chord within you because of something you or a loved one may have personally experienced or are experiencing now. If that is the case, by all means, let the story serve as a catalyst to forge, perhaps, a long overdue dialogue between you and the affected party(ies).

If at any time you find that the stories in this collection are personally offensive, please close the book and **do not** read further. You may return the book to me, along with proof of purchase, for a full refund, minus shipping and handling. Additionally, please address me personally at the address on the copyright page of this book with any concerns you may have about any of the stories in this collection. If you are a Christian reading this book and you become offended, please do not hesitate to contact me personally at the address on the copyright page of this book.

All of that said, I do hope you will find at least one story that you enjoy, or perhaps two. Honestly, would I be pushing it if I hoped for three?

Enjoy the craft!

EXPECTATIONS

"YOU'RE NOT PLAYING MAID AGAIN THIS WEEKEND, ARE YOU, Brianya?"

"It's no big deal, Cinthia. I'd rather they come here and watch the game. This way I won't worry about Darnell driving drunk."

"I guess you're going to let his low-life friends crash on your living room floor again too? I swear, Brianya, you have *got* to be the most gullible person in the world! What's the matter with you? Why do you let him walk all over you? Just because you're fat, Bri, it doesn't mean you can't be picky." Cinthia's words, though well meaning, cut.

"Don't start, okay? I'm tired. I just got in from work and I need to cook, wash, straighten up around here, and get my head on straight to meet his people tomorrow. Darnell will be home in a bit and I want to have dinner at least cooking when he walks in." Brianya filled a pot with water, added a teaspoon of salt, and placed it over the flame.

"Whatever. I can't even believe we came from the same gene pool. What kind of example are you setting for me? If you're trying to get the ring, you're doing it all wrong."

"Look, you worry about getting your own ring and I'll worry about mine. Anyway, I presume you called for a reason." She added olive oil to a skillet, dumped in a package of seasoned ground turkey, added a few spices of her own along with precut mushrooms, bell peppers, and onions, and stirred.

"Yeah, I did call for a reason, but now I don't want to tell you."

"Cinthia, I'm not in the mood for this. Say what you called to say and let me get on with my business."

The pause was too long. What was her little sister up to this time? "Promise you won't get mad at me. I'm just the messenger."

The battery warning on Brianya's phone chirped. "Say it, or I'm hanging up!"

Another long pause. "Ask Darnell about the twenty-dollar bill I picked up. Gotta go. Bye!"

Before Brianya could form a question to shoot back at Cinthia, the line went dead. She pulled the phone away from her ear and stared at it. She hated when Cinthia hung up on her. Ever since her sister was old enough to make speech patterns, she had shown a propensity for the melodramatic. Whatever nonsense she was up to this time, Brianya wouldn't take the bait. The last time she played this cryptic game of cat and mouse with Cinthia, it had almost cost her a lifelong friend.

The sound of footsteps approaching the door quickened Brianya's pace. She liked to have dinner all prepared for Darnell these days when he got in from working ten-hour days as a customer service manager at Target, as he'd been doing for the last three and a half months. Their relationship had taken a heavy hit when he lost his job as assistant manager at one of the big box electronics stores two weeks after they started going out. A female employee had accused him of sexual harassment, which Brianya knew couldn't be true. A black mark like that on his employment record was difficult to explain to prospective employers, so Darnell had given up and lived off the money from his 401(k) for three months. When that ran out, he sold almost all of his possessions to keep from losing the lakefront condominium he leased in downtown Cleveland.

At the three-month mark, their relationship was solid, and Brianya hadn't minded paying his utility bills until he got on his feet. At that point, she had practically moved in; she was there at least four nights out of the week. They may as well make it official, Darnell had said when he asked Brianya to move in.

"It's close to your job. You can even walk to work if you want. Why burn all that gas coming back and forth and then turning around and driving back down here to work? You're probably spending a good two hundred a month in gas alone."

Darnell had a good point. Her lease was up next month. She could use the extra money saved by combining households to help Darnell. "You're right, Darnell. But . . . I don't know. I wasn't raised like that. My family won't like it. My parents are churchgoing, and even though I don't go like I should, I still believe that a man and a woman should be married before they live together."

"When you think about it, we're practically living together already. If we're not spending the night here, then we're at your place. We see each other every day of the week." The desperation in his voice was thick.

It was the dusky hour when the sun turned into a flaming red ball before making its descent and then disappearing behind a curtain of blue sky. They were sitting side by side on the futon that had replaced the expensive sofa he had sold to make partial payments on some credit card debt. Brianya's head rested lightly on Darnell's shoulder. "I do love watching the sunset at your place. And I love waking up next to you," she said breathily into his neck.

Darnell lifted her face and kissed her tenderly. "You can do those things on a more permanent basis."

Her eyes lit up. "How permanent?"

"I think you know what I'm saying." Darnell flashed a hundred-watt smile that creased the corners of his eyes, and Brianya's insides turned to jelly.

All these months later and his smile still had that effect on her. Would he come through on the ring, though? Brianya wondered. As tactless as she was, Cinthia was probably right: Brianya was going about it all wrong.

Brianya finished setting the table just as Darnell shut the door behind him.

"Honey, I'm home!" Darnell said in his best Ricky Ricardo imitation.

"Hey, honey bunny. You got about fifteen minutes before I'm done in here. You remembered to get the wine for tomorrow?" "I got it," he said, coming into the kitchen, kissing Brianya on the back of the neck, and setting the bottle on the counter. "You still cool with the guys coming over Sunday for the game, right?" He grabbed a beer from the refrigerator and leaned against the wall, watching Brianya cook.

"It's good. But you-know-who thinks I need to stop playing maid to you and your 'low-life' friends."

"You-know-who needs to stay out of our business," Darnell said icily. "Bad day at the store, huh?"

Darnell ignored the question.

Brianya added the spaghetti noodles to the pot of boiling water. She yanked her arm back from the hot steam nipping at her forearm.

"I told you to wear those oven mitts I bought when you cook spaghetti. You won't be satisfied unless you burn your whole arm off. Let me see." He took her outstretched arm, examined the area where the steam had caught her, and rubbed gently.

"You know, if you really want to be sweet to me," Brianya said, smiling prettily, "you'll take the salad out of the bag and wash it, add those tomatoes I cut up, and toss it. But first wash your hands."

Darnell did as he was told, frowning as he washed his hands in the sink. Brianya toyed with the idea of broaching the subject of Cinthia's mysterious message but decided it could wait.

***

After eight months, she was finally going to meet Darnell's family. They weren't close like Brianya's family. In fact, they only got together for weddings and funerals. Watching Brianya and her family interact, Darnell said, gave him incentive to want to reach out to his own people. Surprisingly, most of them were open to a family gathering.

The ride to his parents' home in Bedford Heights, an Eastern suburb of Cleveland, was mostly quiet, except for the sounds the tires made as they slapped the asphalt. The walk from the car to the backyard seemed to go on forever. With each step Brianya's stomach did flip-flops, and her palms went clammy and cold.

As they approached a table surrounded by people, Darnell squeezed Brianya's fingers and whispered, "You don't have anything to be nervous about. I'll be right by your side."

Darnell made introductions and chatted easily with family and friends, while Brianya struggled through the awkwardness of making conversation with total strangers. She glanced nervously from one face to the next. So many names and faces to remember, including two new friends she'd never met before—Norris and Calvin. All but one of Darnell's siblings were there. The two who were present were polite. But from the looks in their eyes, Brianya understood what their mouths didn't say: *How did my brother end up with someone like you?*

Brianya caught the almost imperceptible nod Norris directed toward Darnell and saw the two men exchange knowing glances. "What was—" Brianya started to say before Darnell cut her off.

"Will you be all right, baby?" Darnell whispered to Brianya, giving her shoulder a reassuring pat. "I need to go inside for a minute."

"Uh, I guess."

"Make yourself a plate. I'll be right back," he said and rushed off.

Eating was the last thing she wanted to do, but she loved barbecue ribs, and the smell made them too enticing to resist.

When she returned to the table, she could see his family's eyes assessing her. His sister's expression, reprimanding her for piling her plate with food, took her back to the ninth grade. She'd been eating lunch in the cafeteria when Helen Mays, one of the prettiest girls in school, walked up to her and spat on her food. "That ought to keep you from eating so much!" she'd said, and Brianya felt like the whole school was laughing at her.

Brianya quickly dismissed the memory, pushed her plate aside, and concentrated on her surroundings. The backyard easily stretched to two acres, more than enough space to accommodate the small gathering of family and friends. Minutes after Brianya had joined them, Darnell's siblings and friends excused themselves. A woman whom Darnell had introduced as Ma Pearl kept staring at Brianya and the discarded plate of food and smiling. "Eat that food, baby," she said. "We don't believe in waste here. You go on; you got nothing to be ashamed of. I had a daughter who was big just like you. She loved to eat too."

Brianya gave the woman a warm smile and was about to ask about her daughter when Mrs. Jones, Darnell's mother, cut in and started telling her how all the vegetables for the salad came straight from her garden. As Mrs. Jones droned on about gardening, Brianya noticed the striking resemblance between mother and son, from physical features to mannerisms. Later, a lengthy conversation with Mr. Jones revealed that Darnell had inherited his father's gregarious personality. Around the edges, however, there was just a hint of something dark and sad—the way the old man would make a joke and laugh heartily, then almost as quickly turn inward and appear to brood. Brianya had seen that same trait in Darnell when he'd lost his job. A ton of pampering and ego stroking had worked wonders and turned his mood around.

As minutes turned into hours, Brianya glanced anxiously at her watch several times, wondering what was keeping Darnell. Almost two hours had passed since she'd last seen him, and she was starting to feel put upon.

Some cousin whose name she couldn't remember asked Brianya if Mellow Beans Coffee Corporation, where she worked in the human resources department, was hiring. She gave him the usual pat answer about submitting an application online and continued surveying the backyard for any sighting of Darnell. She spotted him huddled with his siblings and the two friends she'd met. Relieved, she hurried over to him.

"Oh. Hey," Darnell said, surprised to see Brianya.

"I was looking for you to come right back." She tried to keep the irritation out of her voice, but some of it managed to leak out.

"Yeah. Uh, I got caught up with something. Did you eat?" The nerve above Darnell's left eyebrow jumped, the way it always did when he was hiding something.

"Everything was delicious," she lied. "I'm a little tired. When do you think you'll be ready to go?"

"I got some things I need to take care of for my dad. It might take a while. Tell you what, you can take my car and go on home. I'll get a ride."

"Is that what you've been doing for the past *two hours?*"

Ten pairs of eyes stared in Darnell's direction. "You know me, Bri," Darnell said, handing Brianya his keys. "Can't say no to someone in need." His voice rose an octave.

Brianya took the keys from Darnell's outstretched hand. She pulled the car key from the ring and pushed the key ring, more forcefully than she intended, into his palm. "I'll see you at home, sweetie." She leaned in and pecked Darnell on the cheek, mostly for show.

The clock on the bedside table read 1:13 a.m. when Brianya heard the jangle from Darnell's keys as he dropped them on the table near the entryway.

***

It was almost eight o'clock when Cinthia deposited Brianya outside her building after they'd spent all day together. Now all Brianya wanted to do was soak in a hot bubble bath and sip on a glass of white wine.

The agreement was that Darnell's friends could watch the game at his place, but they had to be gone by 7:30 since Monday was a workday. The last time his friends had watched a game at the condo, it had turned into a sleepover. She prayed that wouldn't be the case this time.

When she pushed open the door, Brianya gasped. Beer cans and Subway food wrappers littered the living room table. A sticky substance covered a small area on the brand-new sofa they had bought just a month ago. Empty pizza boxes were stacked on the kitchen counter, and someone had ground cigarette butts out in the sink. No friends in sight, though. Thank goodness. If this was the trade-off for having his friends leave at a decent hour, she could live with the mess.

She found Darnell in the bedroom talking on the phone. So engrossed was he in his conversation that he didn't hear her footsteps.

Brianya, arms folded across breasts that were too small for her massive frame, leaned the full weight of her 353 pounds against the doorframe, filling almost every inch of it. Her round eyes narrowed and her heartbeat quickened as she watched and listened.

"I've got a good one for you," she heard him say into the receiver. "What looks like an elephant but eats like a horse?" He paused, waited for an answer, already boisterous laughter escaping from him, then answered his own question. "Brianya!" he bellowed, and roared with laughter.

His laughter was infectious. She laughed too, silently, even though his words stung. That was the umpteenth time she had overheard him making jokes at her expense. She'd heard all the jokes before: the one about her being so fat that when she walked it sounded like the Fourth of July; the one about her being so fat that she'd have to *lose* weight to even be considered obese; and the one that seemed to elicit the most laughter, the one about her behind being so big that when she walked it looked like two dwarves fighting.

The joke about being obese was Darnell's masterpiece. That was the first joke she'd heard him make about her weight. Though it hurt her at first, she eventually laughed too. When she thought about it, she had to admit the jokes were funny. She knew he didn't mean anything by it. Darnell was a kidder; that was what he did. Though she was fat, he didn't mind; he told her that all the time. He said there was just more of her to love. And he did love her—morning, noon, and night. He often remarked that she was the zero to his number one.

Brianya always seemed to attract men with slight builds, and Darnell was no exception. At 5'10", he weighed in just under 157 pounds, which was ideal for his brown swimmer's body. The night they met, an older and more substantially-built, bearded man had chatted Brianya up in the hopes of winning her affections. But like flies to feces, Brianya's curiosity turned toward Darnell, two years younger and half her size, when he had made his move.

"Excuse me, Miss," Darnell had said, approaching the spot at the bar where Brianya and her companion sat. "Can you tell me something?"

Intrigued, Brianya turned her attention to the man standing in front of her, whose body language shouted confidence.

"Why are you wasting your time on strip steak when you can have filet mignon?" he said, tugging on the lapels of his expensive-looking suit.

Brianya burst out laughing. The older man got off his bar stool and got in Darnell's face, warning him to back off. Darnell shrugged his words away and continued speaking to Brianya.

"I knew that if you smiled it would light up the room. I've been watching you all night, and this is the first time I saw you smile. Obviously you're not into this old dude."

The challenging look Darnell gave the man wasn't lost on him. Before slinking away in embarrassment, the man had the gall to drop his business card on the bar and tell Brianya to call him when she was ready for a real man and not a pint-sized perpetrator. He said it low enough so that only Brianya could hear.

"He wasn't the one for you," Darnell said, occupying the vacant seat. "Any man not willing to fight for you ain't worth your time."

"Amen!" Brianya made a show of ripping up the business card. "Now you tell me something," she said, curiosity raising her eyebrows. "What did I do to merit your gallantry?"

Darnell feigned shock. "What? You don't know?" He took her hand in his. "It's not *what* you are but *that* you are," he said, kissing the back of Brianya's hand.

"You just lost cool points," Brianya said and laughed. "I can't remember the last time I laughed this much with a man that I wasn't on a date with."

"For real? We'll have to change that. Stick with me and I'll take you places you've never been. I'll teach you things you don't even know you want to know. Girl, I'll treat you like no man has ever treated you."

That's how the rest of the evening went—exchanges of playful banter. Darnell had changed things for Brianya. She had never been happier, had never laughed as much. Despite not having taken her to places she'd never been or taught her things she didn't know she wanted to know, he did treat her like no man had ever treated her. He loved her unconditionally. If he sometimes got a little carried away with his jokes about her weight, then that was okay; it was a small price to pay. He wasn't perfect either. His forehead was too big. She had joked with him about that, but always in private. He was more sensitive about his flaws than she was about hers; Brianya respected that.

Feeling uncomfortable about eavesdropping on Darnell's conversation, Brianya called out to him.

Startled, Darnell turned around, looking sheepish. "I'll call you later," he said hurriedly into the receiver. He grinned at Brianya as he slammed the phone onto its base. "I didn't even hear you come in. How long were you standing there?"

"Long enough to hear you tell that tired joke." She sighed. "I see your friends still don't have any home training."

"Yeah. Don't worry about that mess. I'll clean it up."

It worried Brianya that Darnell didn't apologize for the joke the way he usually did. His joke telling always followed a pattern: something he saw or heard triggered a memory of Brianya eating, and he would tell a joke. Afterward he'd apologize to her, saying how the joke was just sitting there begging to be told. She always accepted the apology, and they moved on. This time he didn't apologize, and Brianya was afraid to ask why.

An hour later, Darnell had the condo looking habitable again. He parked himself on the dry end of the sofa—the other side was wet from the cleaning solution he'd used to remove the stain—and watched an old episode of Law and Order with the volume high. Ever since the get-together at his parents' home, Darnell's mood seemed off. It wasn't like when he lost his job; this was more of a transitory mood, as if it were a passenger on a bus, waiting for the right stop before it could exit. It had Brianya feeling unsure of herself, afraid to say the wrong thing, feeling out of control. She didn't like it. When she felt out of sorts, she did regrettable things—things that went against her easygoing personality.

"Bri," Darnell said, watching her back as she stood over the dishwasher, emptying its contents. When she didn't answer, he called again, louder.

"I'm not deaf," she said, turning to face Darnell. He had shut off the TV and moved to the dining area. She hadn't noticed the sudden silence. "Didn't mean to shout, but you didn't hear me the first time. Can you bring me something to drink while you're in there?"

"Yeah, give me a sec. I need to finish what I'm doing." Brianya opened a can of pop for Darnell, poured herself a half glass of unsweetened iced tea, and joined him.

"Sit down, Bri," Darnell said and patted the seat cushion on the claw- footed dining chair next to him. "Sweetheart," he said, with a slight rise in the pitch of his otherwise calm voice, "we need to talk."

This can't be good, Brianya thought. Whenever a sentence began with "we need to talk," Brianya was always on the receiving end of a good-bye speech. All the signs were there: the downward pull at the corners of Darnell's mouth and the pulsating vein in his neck. Brianya sat.

"Bri," he began, "you know that I love you and I need you in my life." He stroked the side of her face with the back of his hand; she leaned into him, some of the tension ebbing.

Brianya breathed an inaudible sigh of relief and silently reprimanded herself for not having more faith in Darnell—she had worried for nothing. She couldn't believe he was getting ready to ask her the question that every woman who has given her all to the man she loves dreams of hearing. The first week after they met, Brianya had known that Darnell was her soul mate. No one understood her the way he did. He accepted her wholly and completely. He knew her hopes, her dreams, and her fears. He laughed with her, he cried with her, and now he was about to lay all her fears to rest and make it official. Brianya could hardly contain the girlish giggle tickling the back of her throat.

Darnell locked eyes with Brianya and she was mesmerized, just like the first time he'd looked at her like that, making her feel safe and protected. Releasing her gaze, Darnell clasped her hands in his, gently brushed the tips of his fingers against Brianya's, and said, "I think we need to call it quits, but let's still be friends."

Brianya burst out laughing. "Stop playing, Darnell, and just ask me what I know you wanted to ask me that was so important that you had me sit down."

"I'm serious, Bri. I can't do this anymore." Darnell looked serious. "I need room to breathe. I feel confined."

The can of pop toppled over as Brianya snatched her hands away. Darnell pushed back from the table and went to retrieve the roll of paper towels from above the kitchen sink.

The shadow that passed over and through Brianya left her feeling naked and exposed. She tried desperately to conceal her emotions, but her voice wavered when she spoke. "Can't do what anymore, Darnell?"

"This," he said, turning to face her, making a sweeping gesture with both hands.

"What is *this*?" she mocked. "Do you mean me and you? You can't do this relationship anymore, this life anymore, what?"

"You and me. I can't do you and me anymore."

Brianya's heart tried to find its rhythm. She breathed as deeply as she could and coughed several times, trying to regulate her erratic heartbeat.

"Are you okay?" The panic in Darnell's eyes seemed genuine.

Brianya didn't answer. She coughed a few more times, eventually able to relax, and stared at Darnell in wonder. "Is it because of the weight?"

The words came out choked.

Darnell waited a long beat. "No," he said finally. "Well, yes and no. I can't deal with my friends making jokes about you all the time. I mean . . . It's me, not you, okay? It's just something in me, you know . . . a restlessness. It's hard to explain."

She rose from her chair and stood at the arch of the kitchen entrance. "Well, then explain this: What did Cinthia mean when she told me to ask you about the twenty-dollar bill?" She spat the words at him.

"Ask her what she meant because I don't have a clue!" The familiar nerve above his left eyebrow jumped.

She didn't want this to be true, didn't want to be standing here having this conversation. But just as her sister had predicted he would do, Darnell had lied. "Seriously?" Brianya said, shoulders slumping.

"Like I said, ask your busybody sister." "That's the lie you're sticking with? You're comfortable with that?" She was incredulous.

Only silence from Darnell.

A few years ago Brianya had invested in some blue chip stocks whose payoff should have been substantial. However, she held the stock too long, and her reward was mediocre at best. This moment felt like then. Back then, she was at the mercy of the stock market. Here in her own home, her haven from the storms of life, she controlled what happened. She not only filled the condo with expensive furnishings; she filled it with her essence. Before she moved in, this was just 742 square feet of space that had been stripped down to the bare walls. She made it a home. Their home. Anger rose in Brianya. Darnell had sold her a bill of goods, and one way or another he was going to answer for it.

"So after eight months, this is what I get?" she said, inching closer to Darnell. "Some lame excuse about you being restless and how you can't deal with your friends making jokes about me? Correct me if I'm wrong, Darnell, but didn't I just hear you making a joke about me?" Brianya said, staring at the idiotic expression on Darnell's face. Brianya had learned early on that Darnell hated confrontations. He often used humor as a shield, which was one reason she put up with his jokes.

"Bri—" he started to say but was quickly silenced.

"Uhn-uhn," Brianya said, wagging her index finger in Darnell's face. "You don't get to talk; you get to listen! You're a thirty-two-year-old child, Darnell. I've put up with a lot of crap from you and now it's my turn to talk. I've seen you through one of the lowest periods in your life. I've helped you put your life back in order, even stuck by you when everybody was telling me to walk away. When you couldn't make the rent, pay the utilities, buy groceries, or pay your bills, who paid for you?" She didn't wait for answer. "Me, that's right. And why did I do those things? Because I love you. Oh," she said as if an afterthought. "I also thought—no, scratch that—was led to believe that this relationship was heading somewhere. Somewhere like, oh, say, a more *permanent* arrangement. Oops, my bad; it was all a joke. Am I laughing, Darnell? Do you see me laughing?" She screamed the words only inches from his face.

Hemmed against the kitchen sink, Darnell had nowhere to escape to. He had never seen Brianya this angry. Fear registered in his eyes; he looked like a trapped animal. Her anger reached a crescendo, then plummeted into a valley of calmness. Not good. Brianya pressed her body against Darnell's, reached behind him, and snatched a butcher's knife from the wooden knife block on the countertop. Darnell's head turned toward the sound the knife made as it dislodged from the holder. Brianya pressed him harder against the sink. Reflexively, Darnell caught Brianya's wrist in a vice grip and lowered her hand.

They faced off in a stare down.

Brianya's words cut through the silence. "If you hope to get out of here alive, you *will* tell me about that twenty-dollar bill!" she said through clenched teeth.

The fear left Darnell's eyes, replaced by resignation. "Put the knife down, Bri. I'll tell you." He released Brianya's wrist and pushed against her in an attempt to extricate himself.

Brianya remained glued to the spot. She searched Darnell's eyes for any trace of deceit. Finding none, she pulled back but continued holding the knife. Darnell suggested they sit; Brianya refused. The adrenaline pumping through her had her feeling jittery and restless. Sitting was the last thing she wanted to do.

"Fine. We can stand," Darnell said. He moved away from the sink and stood with his back pressed against the refrigerator. He kept his eye on the knife at Brianya's side.

Loud thumping noises came from the unit above, and the fan on the refrigerator whirred. Sounds of home.

Brianya watched Darnell's expression go through a series of changes before settling on regret. The last time she'd seen that look was when after months of rejection, discouraged and downtrodden, Darnell had given up trying to find work.

She fought the urge to comfort him.

"Well?" she said.

"I'm sorry, Bri," was all he said.

"Oh, no! You'll have to do better than that." She patted the knife against her thigh.

A guttural sound emanated from Darnell. Following a silence that seemed to stretch the length of the Mississippi river, he finally spoke. "Well. . . the other day I was in Walmart with an old friend. The two of them— Cinthia and my friend—were in line. When my friend went to pay, the money fell on the floor and Cinthia picked it up."

"That's it? So my sister is playing a cloak-and-dagger game with me all because she picked up some money that your friend dropped on the floor? I don't think so."

A shrug from Darnell.

"Look, Darnell. I think I've earned the right to know the truth. That's the least you can do in view of the circumstances. I won't beg you, but I will ask you to man up and give me the respect I deserve." The adrenaline high was dissipating, and her body began to relax. Brianya put the knife on the counter.

"My friend's name is Tricia Yancy," he confessed. "She's eight and a half months pregnant."

It took a second for the name to register, but then Brianya did some quick calculations in her mind. Eight months ago she had met Darnell. Two weeks after that a Tricia Yancy had accused Darnell of sexual harassment, thus ending his nine-year career. And three months after she met Darnell, he asked her to move in with him. Something must have happened in that third month. What?

Darnell explained that Tricia had contacted him at the end of her first trimester; by then she had decided she was going to keep the baby. He knew he couldn't afford to keep his condominium and help support Tricia when she moved to Cleveland to be close to him. So he decided to ask Brianya to move in. He and Tricia had met, Darnell said, at a corporate training seminar almost two years ago. Shortly afterward, they started dating long-distance. When the miles between them became an issue, they called it quits. Then eight months and two weeks ago, an opening became available at one of the east side stores. Tricia was in town interviewing for the job in hopes of relocating to Cleveland. For old times' sake, they hooked up one night. Meanwhile, two weeks after the hookup, Darnell met Brianya. Since Darnell was the only senior manager in on the interviewing, his opinion carried the most weight. When he didn't recommend Tricia for the job, she got upset, and that's when she made the bogus sexual harassment allegation.

"Did she have anything to do with you disappearing at your parents' the other day?"

He looked away, unable or unwilling to face Brianya. "Yeah. She had called Norris right before we got there. She was having labor pains, and one of the neighbors took her to the hospital. That's what I was doing in the house—talking to her, trying to calm her down until I could get out there to see about the baby."

Darnell slouched against the refrigerator with his hands in his pockets and looked down at his shoes. "When you left, I went to the hospital. Turns out, it was a false alarm."

Brianya bit back a nasty reply and asked instead, "So why were you in Walmart with her?" On some level, Brianya couldn't believe they were actually having this conversation. It was surreal.

"I had got off work early that day and went with her to her doctor's appointment. Afterward, she wanted to pick up some things from the store, so I made a pit stop before taking her home."

"So you're doing this out of a sense of duty?" She was starting to feel better, even a little bit hopeful about their situation. The baby was his responsibility, after all. He should be a part of its life. That didn't mean that the two of them couldn't still be together. Knowing Darnell the way she did, Brianya was sure that the only reason he wanted to call it quits was because he didn't know how to manage a complicated situation like this. He needed to know that she would never dream of coming between him and his child. What kind of woman would that make her? They could work through this. Admittedly, it would take some getting used to, but it was manageable; people did it all the time.

"Yes," Darnell said in answer to Brianya's question. "I am doing this out of a sense of duty. But I'm also in love with her."

Brianya moved with the agility of someone half her size and grabbed the knife off the counter. Before Darnell had a chance to react, Brianya had the tip of the blade pointed left of center at Darnell's chest.

"You've got to the count of three to get out. And don't come back!"

"B-but this is m-my condo," Darnell protested.

"One . . ." Relieved to hear the slamming door, Brianya dropped the knife on the counter and sank to the floor. She had come close to committing an act that she had no idea she was capable of committing. Just the thought of threatening to do bodily harm to another human being, no less someone she loved, was a violation of who she was. *What if he hadn't left?* she thought. She was thankful that she would never know the answer to that question.

Brianya sat crumpled on the floor, crying rivers of tears, for what felt like an eternity. Finally she dried her eyes, pulled herself up, and went to work. She grabbed a handful of garbage bags and went from room to room, filling them with every item she had purchased. When she was finished with the bathroom and linen closet, nothing was left in them but one worn, blue face cloth and a burgundy bath towel that was there before she moved in. She repeated the process in every room, leaving only what was there before.

Brianya did a final walk-through of the condo, deciding that just for spite she'd leave Darnell a surprise. She dropped his electric toothbrush in the toilet, then poured his expensive aftershave down the sink, and refilled the bottles with tap water.

She glanced into the bedroom on her way back to the living room, making sure she hadn't left any of her personal items behind. Her breath caught when her gaze fell upon the Manhattan platform bed. Just a few nights ago, they had lain lazily in each other's arms, listening as WZAK's *For Lovers Only* played softly in the background and making plans for this week or that as if their world would go on forever. She had seen this movie a thousand times, and each time it ended happily.

Somehow, someone had flipped the script and changed her PG-13 life to an R-rated horror movie and recast her role, without bothering to consult her.

Brianya eyed the eight-by-ten red picture frame that held a photograph they'd had taken while on a dinner dance cruise amid the *GoodTime III*, with stringed lights and endless blackness as the backdrop. She contemplated taking it, decided not to, then turned out the bedroom light and walked out. Eight stuffed garbage bags lined the living room walls. Because she couldn't carry the larger pieces of furniture, she'd have to leave those behind. She would send her brother to pick up the remaining items she'd bought herself.

She rummaged through the junk drawer in the kitchen and found an ink pen and a pad of paper. Brianya wrote out two itemized lists of every big-ticket item they'd bought together. She halved the total (in his favor) and wrote in large letters on the bottom of Darnell's list: "WILL I HAVE TO TAKE YOU TO COURT?"

She put the note and the keys where he was sure to see them and started dragging bags into the hallway to load into her car. Brianya emptied the condo of the last bag, shut off the lights, and walked out, leaving the door unlocked. At almost two o'clock in the morning, she didn't have long to wait for the elevator. The plaintive groans issuing from the elevator as it made its descent from the seventeenth floor echoed Brianya's own feelings. As Brianya inched closer to her destination, she thought about the last thing her sister had said to her before she had dropped her off just hours ago: "If you don't ask him about the money, you may as well change your name to concrete, because you'll be letting him walk all over you." In the recesses of her heart and mind, Brianya knew that Cinthia was right. But a part of her heart—the part that believed in fairy tales and happy endings—didn't want to give up so easily.

She wanted the huge payoff that was supposed to come after her eight- month investment. She'd earned it. Brianya held up her left hand and stared through tears at the naked ring finger. She had chased the ring her whole life, and this was the closest she'd ever come to attaining it—but at what price? Self-respect? Dignity? She had given to Darnell far more than she had to any man. And he had repaid her by stealing her self-worth. She wouldn't let him have it. Only she could determine her value. "I'm better than this!" Brianya said, kicking one of the bags, imagining that it was Darnell. She kept kicking until rivens of plastic, towels, and sheets were strewn across the elevator floor.

The elevator doors opened onto the lobby, and Brianya quickly changed destinations and pressed G for ground. In the trash room, she unloaded the contents of the garbage bags into the dumpster and listened to the purifying sound of her precious items colliding and breaking into irreparable pieces of the past. Every item had memories of Darnell etched into it—memories she was better off without. This was Brianya's opportunity to start over. Unloading the mental baggage wouldn't be easy, she knew. She'd start by rewriting the script to her life. This time, she'd do things the right way.

INNOCENCE

"*NEARLY ONE HUNDRED THOUSAND WOMEN ARE RAPED EVERY year in the United States. Learn how to protect yourself. Up next on the six o'clock news on WKYC channel 3!*"

That news teaser came through my television just as Shelby and I were about to shut off the television and retreat to the kitchen to make my famous chocolate chip cookies, her favorite.

"Mommy, what's rape?" Shelby asked, her small forehead creasing with a concern that no four-year-old should ever have. Her question took me by surprise, and I was momentarily stunned into silence.

"Come here, sweetheart," I said, pulling a yellow plastic chair from under the wobbly, wooden kitchen table. I sat down and put Shelby on my lap. "I don't think that's a subject you're old enough to understand," I said, smoothing a few wisps of hair that had escaped her braids. I wanted to keep her young and innocent for as long as I could. I wanted her to have the childhood that I hadn't been allowed to have. There would be plenty of time for deep subjects.

She stared at me with that pondering look that she sometimes gives me, a look that says she understands a lot more than I give her credit for. She frowned as she played with the gold filigree hoop earrings that dangled from my earlobes. Then she rested one tiny brown hand on my shoulder. "Mommy, the news man said that we have to protect ourselves. And that's what you said too. Right?"

"Yes, baby, Mommy did say that." I could see there was no putting her off. I would have to give her the G-rated definition in terms that her young mind could comprehend. Children's minds are like sponges: they hold on to information until you squeeze them and your own words come pouring out of their mouths like water. Shelby was right. I was always telling her that she should be aware of what was going on around her, not talk to strangers, not let anyone touch her, and scream if she even *thought* someone was going to do something bad to her. We even had practice sessions at home, where I played the "bad person." Shelby was an excellent student; she always remembered and knew all the right things to do. I could only pray that if she was ever confronted with a real-life situation, she would remember everything I'd taught her.

Rather than let a news program teach my child about one of the most horrific injustices a person could endure, I put Shelby down, went into the sitting room, pulled the encyclopedia off the bookshelf, and returned to the kitchen. Shelby hopped up on my lap and began thumbing through the colorful pages of the encyclopedia. The earlier conversations we'd had about the female and male genitalia really came in handy! But after about five minutes of talking about that, Shelby was growing restless; I think she knew that I was stalling.

"Mommy, you told me all that before," she said, a trifle impatient. "What's rape?"

"Rape," I said, swallowing hard, "is when a man puts his. . . ." Oh dear God, I couldn't finish. How could I explain such a horrible, violent crime to my sweet, pure child? If I did, I would be stealing part of her childhood, forcing her to grow up faster than she should have to. Without realizing it, I was crying. The look of alarm on Shelby's face and her own tears told me what I needed to know: she was too young for this conversation.

Shelby patted and stroked my hand, cooing softly that everything was going to be all right, something I had done with her many times when she cried or was afraid to sleep in her bed because the shadows on the walls looked like big men. "It's gonna be okay, Mommy. Let it all out. You feel better," she said, parroting me.

The sweet little way she was talking to me made my heart swell and renewed my determination to protect her from harm at any cost. She wrapped her little arms around my neck, kissed the wetness on my cheeks, and told me that she loved me and that she wouldn't let anything bad happen to me. "I love you, Mommy," she said, and added words she'd heard me often say to her: "You my rock!"

I squeezed her in return and repeated the words back to her. I couldn't imagine what life would be without her, and I didn't ever want to find out.

Later that night when I was putting Shelby to bed, the subject of rape came up again. With a child's naïveté, Shelby blurted out, "Mommy, did you get raped?"

Her words went through me like cannonballs and my throat constricted. I grabbed Shelby and squeezed her in a long embrace, stroking her back, as if she were a sick child in need of comfort. This time I didn't want her to see the tears; I didn't want my child to know that I was coming undone.

"I'm sorry, Mommy, I'm sorry!" Shelby shrieked, breaking free from my grasp. "I won't rape you, Mommy, I promise!" Her small face was terror-stricken, and I felt helpless.

The forcefulness and absurdity of her words tore at me. What was I doing to my child; what burden was I saddling her with? I folded her in my arms, this time more gently, and cooed reassuring words in her ear, assuring her that she could never do something so terrible to me. I was forced then to explain to her just what rape is, leaving out the most graphic descriptions. I spoke of the subject in the most clinical of terms, just the way the doctors and police officers had spoken to me five years ago when I was found in an abandoned building, teetering halfway between life and death, and taken to the nearest hospital.

Out of the most heinous of crimes had come a blessing that has surpassed anything I could ever imagine in life. My child will never know the circumstances of her conception. As long as I live, no one will ever stigmatize her as a "rape baby." As far as anyone knows, her father is a man I had been dating but had broken up with shortly before the rape. It was easy to conceal the rape by blaming my ex because he was a violent man and had gotten physical with me a few times. I never wanted to relive that horrifying night, and I didn't want Shelby to feel one iota of shame because of it. If I had to lie, cheat, and steal to keep the truth from my child, I would do it. For now, the subject would rest, but I knew it would come up again. The next time, however, I would be ready for it.

Shelby had finally calmed down; she lay limp in my arms, heavy with sleep. I placed her gently in the middle of her bed, shut off the light, and curled next to her in the small bed, both of us secure in the knowledge that we would always have each other.

CAUGHT

LONNIE PARKER PEERED INTO THE BATHROOM MIRROR AT the puffy sacks taking up residence beneath his walnut-colored eyes. He couldn't sleep. His once flawless bronze skin seemed to have aged over the past three months. Was that a gray hair residing at his temple? His hair was already cut close to his scalp; he thought maybe he should shave it all off. Lonnie rubbed his tired, sleepless eyes and sighed heavily before dousing his face with frigid water. He shivered as a chill ran through his tall, solid body. His muscles felt taut; he needed to find a way to relax. Until he resolved this situation, he would feel no relief. He stretched, yawned, and rubbed his eyes with the palms of his hands. How often could he keep dodging the same bullet?

Juanna, his current muse, wasn't the first one to use the pregnancy ploy. However, she was the first to produce tangible evidence—as tangible as any positive pregnancy test from a doctor's office could be. Lonnie wasn't willing to accept Juanna's word that the baby was his, so she suggested a prenatal amniocentesis DNA test. The test was costly, but since Lonnie wanted—needed—to know the answer, he agreed to pay for the testing. Two weeks ago, when she entered her fourteenth week of pregnancy, they had the test done. Yesterday the results had revealed with 99.7 percent certainty that Lonnie was the biological father. He was caught.

Juanna was typical of the type of women Lonnie had been hooking up with lately: women with issues. She should have been a one-night stand, but the gentle caresses from the long, slender fingers on her pretty hands and the sweetness of her sexy voice made him stay too long. By the time morning rolled around, she had him so hooked that he had a real date with her scheduled in his Blackberry. When the spell finally broke, it was too late. Now, in light of this recent development, breaking up with her wasn't going to be easy. What Lonnie had hoped to avoid, he couldn't. Juanna was a friend of a friend, and breaking up with her now would hurt her; and hurting Juanna meant having to deal with his friend—something he didn't want to have to do just yet.

Juanna was determined to get Lonnie to marry her, but marriage was definitely not in his plans. Watching his parents' loveless marriage explode into brutal rages with frequent bouts of domestic violence had put a determination in him that was ironclad: children and marriage were definitely not for him.

His father would come home from a night of heavy drinking and gambling upset that he had lost most of his paycheck shooting craps, playing poker, or whatever other game of chance fancied him—Edwin was forever looking for easy money. As usual, he would stumble into the apartment long after Lonnie and his siblings were in bed for the night. Lonnie and his older brother Horace were light sleepers, so they always witnessed the buildup of anger that inevitably led to their mother cowering in some corner of the apartment with her lip split or her body covered in welts that looked like long, angry worms crawling over her arms and legs and probably other parts of her body they couldn't see.

One July night, the heat index still hovering at 90, even at midnight, Lonnie and Horace sat on their beds in the dark, long past their bedtime, rehashing the plan they had devised earlier in the week to stop their father from abusing their mother and them.

"Remember, Lonnie, wait till you hear Dad get loud before you run into the bedroom. I'll be right behind you with the brick. Just stand in the middle of them. Keep Dad's back to the door so I can sneak up on him," Horace said. "Don't be scared!" he added.

Lonnie could hear the fear in his brother's words, and it scared him. Horace, age seventeen, four years older than Lonnie, hated his father a lot more than Lonnie did. Lonnie supposed that made sense, since Horace had endured their father's abuse a lot longer than he had. He hoped the fear in Horace's voice didn't mean he was having doubts about the plan.

"I know my part," Lonnie said, projecting bass into his voice. "Just make sure you get there before he comes after me. You got the brick?"

Two streets over from where they lived, the city of Cleveland had demolished two dilapidated apartment buildings that had sat abandoned for nearly three years. Every day on the way home from school, Horace and Lonnie had waited for a chance to jump the fence and take one of the bricks. Yesterday, they got their chance.

"Yeah, I got it," Horace said defensively.

The room smelled of unwashed feet and of fear. Sweat trickled from Lonnie's armpits. Lonnie quickly wiped the moisture away with the corner of his sheet, afraid that Horace would interpret the sweat as fear.

"You good?" Horace asked, as if he had read Lonnie's mind.

"Uh-huh," Lonnie said, and just then they heard the squeak of the front door. Both boys sat up straight. They stilled themselves, afraid to move.

Horace was the first to rally into action. "Go!" he said, pushing Lonnie toward the bathroom where he would wait for his cue.

From the bathroom door, Lonnie could see the digital clock on the microwave in the kitchen. Five minutes went by . . . ten . . . twelve. When twenty minutes had passed, Lonnie became hopeful that maybe his father had finally followed through on his promise to stop drinking and gambling. At the twenty-two minute mark, Lonnie didn't hear the raised voice of his father; he heard movement. Scuffling sounds. The sound of leather hitting flesh. Thwack!

Lonnie sprang into action. He burst into the bedroom. His father, belt raised high, stood over his mother, who was balled up and whimpering in a corner of the room. With lightning speed, Lonnie interjected himself between his parents. He was tall for his age and too thin. He had never before stood up to his father, who was a big man—not fat but husky and strong. Lonnie's knees went slack, and he almost lost his balance.

His mother's eyes were wide with concern for her son. "Get outta here, Lonnie! Go back to bed!" she said in a frantic whisper.

Lonnie stood his ground. His father brought the belt down hard against his cheek. Lonnie's skin opened up and blood seeped out. He winced in pain and let out a yelp. He refused to cry. His father would like that, he thought.

Edwin was poised to land another blow, but Mattie sprang to her feet to protect her son. As she did, she caught sight of Horace charging into the room, holding the brick high in the air, ready to pounce, and she cried out, causing Edwin to turn toward the object of his wife's distress.

Horace brought the brick down hard across his father's shoulder, but not hard enough to incapacitate him. Edwin managed to rend the brick from his son's hand. Lonnie and his mother shouted in unison for Edwin to put the brick down.

He didn't.

When he finally did drop the brick, it was covered in blood, and Horace lay on the floor, unmoving.

That was the last time Lonnie had seen his father. Over the years he had tried not to think about him, and for the most part he'd been successful. However, he now had a situation of monumental importance hanging over his head that was causing him to have to dredge up memories and old wounds, and there was no getting around dealing with it. Dealing with the situation meant that he had to explain constantly to Juanna why marriage was out of the question. How many ways could he explain that what she was asking of him was impossible?

The woman lying in his king-sized bed stirred. She was beautiful. She had legs for days and a backside made for hauling cargo. She wore her auburn-colored hair long, just the way Lonnie liked it. She had sensuous lips and a penetrating gaze, both of which she knew how to use to get her way with Lonnie. And she was tall too, almost as tall as Lonnie who was 6' 2".

Lonnie thought about waking her but quickly changed his mind. She would want to talk about "the baby," at which point they would argue. He was tired of arguing with her. When they'd gotten the results back from the prenatal paternity test they had done two weeks ago, Lonnie promised Juanna that he would take care of the baby. He'd thought that would be enough to put her mind at ease and stop all the bickering, but it wasn't good enough. She wanted the whole package. Out of the question. He couldn't marry someone he didn't love. Although he had never been in love, Lonnie knew that what they had wasn't it. How could he love a woman whose only positive attributes were physical? Besides, he didn't really know her. They had only been dating for five months. It had taken him longer than that to decide whether to grow a mustache.

Her presence alone was stifling. He had to get her out of his apartment before she decided to rearrange her schedule and linger all day. Lonnie glanced at the glowing digits on the clock on the nightstand. It read 5:30 a.m. Two hours before the alarm was due to go off.

Juanna opened her eyes, squinted up at Lonnie, and bolted out of bed, almost knocking him over as she pushed past him to get to the bathroom. The familiar sounds of puking and gagging tugged at Lonnie's heartstrings. He knelt down next to Juanna on the bathroom floor and rubbed the small of her back with one hand while holding back her hair with his other hand.

"How much longer will you be doing that?" Lonnie said when she'd finished and leaned her head on his shoulder.

"I don't know. I read that some women have morning sickness all throughout their pregnancy," she said, rubbing her forehead. She made a move to get up. "I need crackers."

Lonnie helped Juanna up from the floor. While she rinsed her mouth with warm water, Lonnie went to the kitchen to get the saltine crackers he made sure to always have on hand.

"I feel sorry for you women," he said, reentering the room and continuing the conversation. He opened a package of the crackers, took out a handful, and handed them to Juanna.

"Yeah. We go through all the agony, and all you men do is sit back and take all the credit." She took the saltines from Lonnie and jammed two into her mouth. She pushed past him into the bedroom and snuggled back under the chocolate-colored satin down comforter.

Lonnie watched Juanna chew the crackers and was reminded of a date gone wrong. Juanna had expressed to Lonnie that she'd like to go to John Q's Steakhouse in downtown Cleveland, so he'd made a reservation and decided to surprise her one Friday night. "Remember the reservation fiasco?"

Juanna looked at Lonnie with a mixture of confusion and playfulness. "Cheapskate!" she said and laughed. "You know you still owe me."

Lonnie laughed heartily. "Hey, I wasn't the one who just had to make that last-minute hair appointment."

They had arrived thirty minutes late for their dinner reservation and couldn't be accommodated because a huge convention was being held in downtown Cleveland and almost all the restaurants were booked solid. Not only had they missed their reservation, but Lonnie had forgotten to grab his wallet off the dresser. Between them they had only $4.52. They ended up going to a Wendy's restaurant close to where Juanna lived in Richmond Heights and ordering dinner from the dollar menu; she got a chili and lots of crackers.

Their relationship was carefree and fun in those days, the way new relationships tend to be—each person feeling out the other, learning boundaries, making pros and cons columns, and deciding whether to stay or go. He could tell at that point that Juanna was getting too comfortable, but she mesmerized him, and he thought he might try staying put. A week later, however, she dropped the pregnancy bomb on him, and that changed things. It was too late, but he chastised himself anyway for betraying his motto: "Love 'em, leave 'em, neva look back."

The room had gone quiet. A slight chill filled the air, along with the faint lingering odor of the White Diamonds perfume Juanna loved so much. He was lost in thought and hadn't heard Juanna the first time.

"What?" he said, coming out of his reverie.

"I said you're staring at me. What are you thinking about?"

He wasn't aware that he'd been staring. "I was just thinking about what my son will look like. . . .What, I can't wonder?" Lonnie said when Juanna didn't acknowledge his answer.

"You can wonder, but you know how I feel."

He knew. If he didn't agree to marry her, she would get rid of the baby. And in Lonnie's opinion, any woman who would do that to a child should be prosecuted for murder. He'd seen the pictures of aborted babies on the Internet a few years ago when the sister he was closest to had done that to her baby. Their relationship was never the same after that. Although he didn't want children for himself, Lonnie loved children, especially his nieces and nephews.

Plans never went as they should. Now that the possibility of fatherhood was an arm's length away, Lonnie was growing accustomed to this impending change in his life. It angered him that Juanna could be so callous about a human life.

Lonnie sat on the edge of the king-sized bed and faced Juanna, looking her directly in the eyes. "I'm going to take care of what's mine, Juanna. You don't have anything to worry about," he reassured her yet again.

Juanna abruptly sat up. "How do I know that, Lonnie? For all I know, I could have this baby, and you would hightail your behind right out of my life."

"Or I wouldn't," Lonnie said matter-of-factly. "The point is, neither one of us knows what's going to happen from one day to the next. And whether we're a couple or not, that child will always be mine, and I'll always provide for what's mine." He was not like his father, who had given Lonnie's mother exactly zero dollars for the four children he was still financially responsible for after he left. Had it not been for state assistance and the charity of family and friends, they would have ended up homeless and hungry.

"That's just it, Lonnie; we *don't* know. But I will tell you this: I'm not bringing a child into this world unless I have a ring on my finger."

"See, there you go with that again, trying to corner me into marrying you. You know how I feel about . . . I'm not feeling that!" He couldn't even bring himself to say the word *abortion*. Lonnie stood and paced the length of the room. "What are you trying to prove, Juanna? Why do you want to marry a man who doesn't love you?" He stopped pacing and faced her.

"I'm not talking about love; I'm talking about making a home for our child. To be honest, Lonnie, I'm not head-over-heels in love with you either, but that'll come in time."

"What kind of atmosphere is that to bring a child into? Children aren't stupid. They know when something is up with their parents. You're talking crazy!"

Juanna hopped up out of bed and jumped in Lonnie's face. "Who are you calling crazy?"

"Come on now, J, don't start with the melodramatics. You know I wasn't calling you crazy." *Umph! She sure is sexy when she's mad*, he thought. Juanna was so close that Lonnie could smell the crackers on her breath. He pulled her to him and wrapped her svelte body in his arms, then ran his thumb down the side of her face. Juanna relaxed. "Look, baby," he said, pressing his nose to hers, "if you don't believe I'll keep my word about taking care of the baby, we can do everything legally. You're going to law school; you know the value of a legal document. I'll put it in writing that I acknowledge that the baby is mine and that I'll provide for him morally, spiritually, financially, the whole gamut. Come on, J, you know I'll do it. Do you really think I would father a child and turn my back on it? I'm asking you to do this for our child, for me."

"Look, Lonnie, you know that my mother died in childbirth and I've been in and out of foster homes my whole life. I know what can happen when children are raised by strangers." The exasperation in her voice came across loud and clear. Juanna stepped out of Lonnie's embrace and turned away. "So are you saying you're *not* going to marry me?"

It was like talking to concrete. Was she so thickheaded that she couldn't understand? Lonnie patiently explained as if he were talking to a very small child. "How can I make you understand, Juanna? When I say 'I do,' love has got to be in the equation; it's a forever deal for me. And if I marry you, I'm telling you flat out right now that I'm not going to be faithful to you, because I don't love you. I would never want to do you the way my father did my mother. He had a different woman every other month. You know that. We talked about all this before." That was the one area where Lonnie's life and his father's resembled each other. He had no idea what his father's number was, but in his short lifetime of twenty-eight years, Lonnie had been with over two hundred women. "Anyway," he said, "you should never settle for a marriage just for the sake of being married. I don't plan to." Lonnie ran his hand across his face. "I'm begging you, Juanna, don't kill my baby. Don't do this!" He had never begged a woman for anything; it felt unnatural, strange. But if his begging spared his son's life, then it was worth it.

Juanna's expression was blank as she began pulling the sheets off the bed. She watched Lonnie out of the corner of her eye. "Look, Lonnie, there's no place in my life for a baby right now. I'm trying to finish law school; I'm working two part-time jobs. I can't take a chance on you going back on your word. I know you keep saying you'll take care of what's yours, but those are just words, paper or no paper." She tossed the sheets in a heap at the foot of the bed, grabbed the pillows, and began shaking them out of the pillowcases. "I don't mean to sound callous, but I'm trying to keep my life clutter free. A baby would clutter up my life. Sorry, Lonnie. I gotta do what I gotta do," she said, tossing the pillowcases into the pile with the sheets.

Lonnie started pacing again, eyes blinking rapidly, swallowing hard, trying to figure out what to do. No matter what he said,

Juanna was determined to have things her way. What kind of life would their child have living in a home where his parents didn't love each other? Children can sense things like that. Lonnie had known at a very young age that his parents' relationship was off. He couldn't put his child through that. He'd rather raise the child alone than subject him to that kind of life.

One way or another, he had to get through to her. "Foster homes may not have been ideal for you, J. But at least your mother didn't kill you—because that's what you're doing. You're taking a life. Whether you want to admit it or not, I know you've felt him move inside you. I've seen you flinch and rub your belly when you didn't know I was looking."

She looked at him, surprised.

"You don't think I'm serious about this but you're wrong. I've been doing research. I also know what happens to babies when you abort them. Have you ever seen one, J—an aborted baby?"

She didn't answer.

He kept talking. Maybe he could tap some deep emotional reserve she kept hidden in the recesses of her heart. "At your stage in the game, sixteen weeks, they have to pull it out piece by piece. Then they take all those discarded pieces and throw them in the trash with the rest of the garbage. Is that what your baby is to you, Juanna—garbage?"

Her eyes widened slightly; however, she remained silent as she went into the bathroom and ran the shower. Lonnie wondered if his words had any effect on her whatsoever. Before she closed the door, he saw the tears that stained her cheeks.

A half hour later, Juanna emerged from the bathroom fully dressed and looking refreshed. The expensive designer handbag that Lonnie had bought her for her birthday three weeks ago lay casually on the floor beside the dresser, where Juanna had tossed it the night before; she now retrieved it and slung the strap over her shoulder. "Lonnie, I know you think I'm being cold-hearted and unfeeling . . ."

"It's my baby too!" he blurted out, not wanting to hear any more of her selfish reasonings. He began pacing again and rubbing his head. If he didn't get a grip on his emotions, his asthma might flare up, and Juanna would see him as sickly and weak, less of a man. Lonnie stopped pacing, walked to the table beside the bed where the phone sat, furiously scrawled out a promissory note, and thrust it in Juanna's face. "I'll give you this much money if you have the baby and give me custody," he said desperately.

"So you could raise him with some strange woman?" Juanna snatched the paper out of Lonnie's hand, appeared to contemplate the offer seriously, and then stared him directly in the eyes. Her expression held no trace of understanding, not a hint of acquiescence. "You just don't get it, Lonnie," she said, shaking her head, disgust written all over her face. "You can kiss this baby good-bye!" she said and walked out of the apartment, slamming the door loudly behind her.

***

Later that night he had concluded that he had to give her what she wanted. He couldn't bear the thought of something made of his flesh and blood undergoing a tragic death with its arms, legs, and torso torn into chunks.

He would agree to marry her, but it would only be temporary, just until the baby was born and he could sue for custody, although she didn't have to know that. Lonnie was serious when he told Juanna that he would cheat on her. He didn't want his son growing up witnessing that.

Lonnie had tried unsuccessfully to get in touch with Juanna for two days, but the calls kept rolling to voice mail. Tired of leaving messages that went unanswered, Lonnie went to her apartment several times, but silence and darkness greeted him each time. It was as if she'd fallen off the face of the earth. He had even waited outside the college, hoping to catch her on her way to or from class. Nothing.

An hour ago Juanna had finally called to say she was on her way over to his apartment. "We need to straighten out some things. I'm on my way over," were her exact words.

Two hours later Lonnie found himself standing in the middle of his living room, going tit for tat with Sharin, the very friend he didn't want to have to deal with. The expletives and descriptive gesturing she'd just unleashed were enough to make even Richard Pryor blush.

"Sharin, you need to mind your own business! This is between me and Juanna!" he shot back.

Lonnie had known Sharin for twelve years, and he had never seen her behave like this. They met as juniors at John Marshall High School, and their mutual messed-up family situations had drawn them close. It wasn't long before they started dating. After high school, however, things cooled off, and they fell back into friendship mode. Sharin had gone to college out of state while

Lonnie did his thing, which consisted of women, an occasional class at Cleveland State University, and more women.

Lonnie stared furiously at his longtime friend, whose head, twisting this way and that, looked like it would come flying off any minute. "Juanna's business is my business!" she shouted. "That's my best friend. When you hooked up with her after the wedding, I told you if you hurt her, you would have to deal with me! Didn't I tell you that?"

"I don't care what you said. But I know you better back up off me and get up out of my face."

"Or what—you'll hit me?"

Juanna, sitting at Lonnie's kitchen table with her hands folded, said nothing. *Just like a typical woman*, Lonnie thought. *Get some mess started, then call in her girl for reinforcement.*

Lonnie moved with lightning speed to the door, twisted the doorknob, and pulled the door wide open. "Get out, Sharin, and take your friend with you!"

At this Juanna met him toe-to-toe, eye-to-eye. "You're not going to give me your half of the money for the abortion?"

Lonnie eyeballed her right back, unblinking, his expression one of disbelief. "I'm not paying for an abortion."

He knew Juanna could be manipulative, but he didn't really believe she would go this far. She was in his apartment eyeballing him and breathing down his neck about him going half on a murder? If it weren't for what his mother and grandmother had taught him about walking away from a woman rather than hitting her and his own personal belief that any man who hit a woman was a coward, Lonnie would have seriously put a hurting on her. And mouth-almighty, tongue-everlasting Sharin wasn't making things any better. She always did talk too much.

Sharin had stepped into the hall, and Juanna's body was halfway in, halfway out of Lonnie's apartment. Lonnie moved forward, forcing Juanna to move backward out of his apartment. "Go to hell, Juanna!" Lonnie said, slamming the door so hard that the mirror hanging on the opposite wall fell to the floor and shattered into pieces.

Lonnie sidestepped the glass shards and retrieved the broom from the hook on the kitchen wall. He didn't realize his jaw was clenched tightly until his head started throbbing.

What gave Juanna the right to make a decision like that without considering his feelings? Lonnie swept pieces of glass into the dustpan. All of his talking and pleading had fallen on deaf ears. *The father's feelings don't matter*, Lonnie fumed. *Women think that because they're the ones who get pregnant, that gives them the right to do whatever they want with the babies.*

Lonnie angrily dumped the dustpan full of glass shards into the garbage can. *They're wrong!* his mind screamed. *Fathers should also have a say. Until women start producing sperm and impregnating themselves, they need to realize that men's feelings count too. Women like Juanna, who take the lives of innocent unborn children, need to be punished swiftly*, Lonnie thought, wiping away the tears that fell from his eyes. He wanted desperately to hurt Juanna, and he knew that if he didn't get a grip on his emotions, he might go chasing after her and do something seriously foul. He needed to de-stress, and quickly.

Lonnie hurriedly put on his running gear and slammed the door behind him as he headed for the Metro parks. A 5-mile run would help to alleviate the intense feelings of hatred he was feeling toward Juanna.

***

As Lonnie changed out of his running gear and prepared to take a shower, he pondered how this pregnancy scare had him rethinking his whole lifestyle.

After a nice long, hot shower, Lonnie had come to a decision. If it weren't for his player ways, he would never have gotten himself into this situation. And he wouldn't have to be dealing with living with the knowledge that he was responsible for an innocent child losing its life. There was only one way to make sure that he would never have to go through this again, Lonnie thought. It was time to turn in his player's card.

E-MALE

SUBJECT: LAST NIGHT
From: "Michael Adams" <boing@funmail.com>
Date: Mon 2/5/07 6:50:44 A.M.
To: "Rita Collier" <R.Collier@Hemphilstores.com>

Good morning, sunshine ☺. Last night was the bomb! I think we must have set a new record for the longest lovemaking session in the world. Girl, I didn't know that you had a li'l freak in you! I like that thing you did with your tongue. Let's hook up tonight. Hit me on the hip when you get this.

Mike

Without a moment's hesitation, Rita Collier pointed the cursor to the delete icon and mashed the button hard, obliterating any vestige of the offensive message. She stared with incredulity at the blank screen of her Dell monitor. *Who would send her such garbage?* she wondered. Surely, this must be a joke. She was a good Christian woman and under no circumstances would she ever behave with such reckless abandon with a man.

"Ugh!" she said under her breath. *That is what is wrong with the world now: men and women do not respect each other; thus, they do not respect themselves*, Rita thought.

Rita knew all about disrespect. In fact, before she got saved she was probably the foremost sinner in that regard. She and several of her coworkers would frequent nightclubs and bars in search of a good time, which more often than not would result in one if not all of them leaving with men who an hour or so earlier were complete strangers. Although Rita had given up that shameful lifestyle, her coworkers had not. "What a pity," she'd often remark.

Rita was no nun, of course. She had desires and needs like any woman; however, she was no longer willing to settle for just any man. The man she would be with had to be saved also, and his life more than his words had to demonstrate that.

Rita wondered what sort of man this Michael person was. Probably the playboy type. She'd certainly had her share of that type of man; it was just that sort that had caused her to seek the comfort of God's merciful embrace. Fed up with ill treatment from her sometimes abusive boyfriend, Eric, and at the insistence of her mother, Rita had gone to church. The sermon that day had been about Jesus and the woman at the well. Though Rita didn't immediately change her lifestyle, she did make it her goal to attend church every Sunday, a goal she had maintained for five years. She was determined not to be an Easter-and-Christmas Christian. She believed that God had worked through her mother and that it was God's will that she be there on that particular Sunday.

An arbitrary thought interrupted Rita's justification routine and she inhaled sharply. Suppose the mysterious man who had sent her that vulgar e-mail was half of a couple who were meant to be together, destined even, and that it was she whom God had chosen to . . . to what? Save them? Yes, that must be it. Why else would she have received the e-mail? If only she hadn't deleted the message. There was no way to retrieve it.

Rita quickly shot off an e-mail to Jaki, her co-worker across the aisle. While it would have been just as easy to walk the ten steps to Jaki's cubicle, Rita didn't want to risk being caught socializing by Mrs. Marbury, her boss.

Rita had worked in the National Accounts Department at Hemphil Department stores for eleven years. And for just as long, she had disliked her boss. She was so exacting, so demanding, and quite unreasonable in her expectations of Rita—so unlike Jesus, who was patient and understanding. Mrs. Marbury expected Rita to be working every minute of the day, except for her lunch. Rita suspected that if Mrs. Marbury had her way, Rita wouldn't even get a lunch break.

When Jaki didn't respond right away to Rita's e-mail, Rita decided to risk the wrath of Mrs. Marbury and suffer the consequences. This was much too important.

Psst! Rita whispered, barely audible, snaking her head around the white, makeshift corkboard wall that served as a divider between desks. Jaki showed no signs of having heard her. *Psst!* Rita said again, this time a decibel louder.

Jaki held up a single finger, petitioning Rita to wait.

Rita craned her neck, trying to make out what Jaki was concentrating on so attentively, but she couldn't.

"I just read your e-mail, girl!" Jaki said and rolled her eyes playfully. "You know something? You need help!"

The two women grinned, stifling laughter.

"Well, it's true, Jaki. What sort of man writes stuff like that in an e-mail message?"

"You'd be surprised. But writing it doesn't make him a pervert."

"Humph! It does in my book!" Rita twisted her lips into a sneer and sighed. "You need Jesus!" she said, only half joking.

"Rita, don't start that. It's too early on a Monday morning, and I don't feel like hearing it." Jaki stood, stretched her long legs, the envy of many women, and yawned. "Come on, let's take a bathroom break."

Rita let the comment slide, knowing that sometimes silence was the best answer. She grabbed her pocketbook from the bottom drawer and followed Jaki to the rest room, where they could talk more freely.

"So what do you think I should have done, Jaki?" Rita peered at her face in the mirror: latte complexion; large, inquisitive eyes with coal-black irises; small button nose; full lips. She knew it was prideful to admire her own attractiveness, but she always had.

"Well," Jaki said, bending to check the stalls and make sure they were alone. "If I were you, I would have e-mailed him back." Jaki rescued a tube of smoky plum lipstick from her overcrowded purse and dabbed some on her thin lips. "Besides, girl, he could be cute." She smoothed her arched eyebrows.

"You *would* do something like that," Rita said, pulling a boar-bristle brush and fine-tooth comb from her pocketbook and placing them on the vanity.

"What do you mean by that?" Jaki spat, eyes narrowed.

Rita hesitated. If she hadn't known Jaki for ten years, she would have terminated their friendship long ago. But Jaki had proved herself a true friend, over and above what Rita had ever expected of a friendship. They had been through a lot together. When Rita had fled from Eric, it was Jaki who had provided a haven for her. Even though Jaki had a propensity to attract men who were of the lowest moral fiber, she was a good matchmaker for other people. Jaki had never once introduced her to anyone. She probably didn't know any upstanding, morally principled men.

"I'm waiting," Jaki said, tapping her foot and drumming her nails on the vanity.

"Well, Jaki, it's not like you . . . You're not the most . . .Oh, heck, Jaki.

You don't have any morals. You keep company with all sorts of disreputable people. You've slept with every man you've ever met. All the men I've tried to set you up with you've found something wrong with. Personally, I think you didn't like them because they were too good. I bet you don't know one decent Christian man. Oh, and you're becoming selfish, Jaki. You never do anything for anyone anymore unless there's something in it for you. Life is not about what you can get out of it; it's about unselfishly giving of yourself to help make someone else's world a little brighter." Rita drew a deep breath, exhaled sharply, parted her hair on one side, and began brushing her freshly relaxed shoulder-length mane with rapid strokes. "Furthermore, not all preachers are 'money-grubbing pimps with their hands deep in the members' pockets,' as you claim. There, I've said it; it's out."

Jaki's eyes moistened and her dark brown complexion turned an even deeper shade of brown.

Rita braced herself; she knew that when Jaki cried, it wasn't because she was sad. No doubt, Jaki would unleash some mean-spirited comment in retaliation, even though Rita's own comments were made in the utmost spirit of love. Rita squared her shoulders with determination. *Well, Jaki will just have to be upset with me,* Rita thought. *I said what needed saying.*

A tear crawled down Jaki's cheek. She pointed a heavily manicured finger in Rita's face and leveled her gaze. "I've had it with you and your sanctimonious, holier-than-thou attitude. You think that just because you go to church every Sunday that makes you a good person. Well, you're wrong. I'm a better person not going to church than you'd ever be if you went twenty-four-seven. At least I keep it real!" Jaki turned to leave, put out a hand to open the door, but stopped. "Oh, one more thing," she said, pushing the door wide open. "You can chill with that bourgeois prim and proper act, too. Everybody knows you're from the 'hood." With that said, Jaki stormed out of the restroom, leaving Rita in wide-eyed shock.

Well, thought Rita, that's that! If Jaki wanted to be thin-skinned about the whole thing, so be it. It wasn't Rita's fault that Jaki was the way she was. The woman was an opportunist with no morals, plain and simple. Respect begot respect, and if Jaki acted respectably, other people would take her seriously and treat her with respect. Rita was sure of that, because if Jaki had taken the time to befriend respect, she would never have behaved as badly as she had a few years back when they had witnessed the tail end of a coworker breaking up with her boyfriend. Instead of consoling her, as Rita had, or as any decent person would have, Jaki had unashamedly asked the woman if it was all right with her if she gave the woman's ex a call . To Rita's surprise and repulsion, the woman had told Jaki to be her guest.

That was when Rita had made it her business to help Jaki reform her life. She had invited Jaki to come to church with her, but Jaki had always made some excuse. Rita knew the real reason Jaki wouldn't go with her was because once Jaki set foot in the Lord's house, she would have to leave her heathen ways at the door, and she wasn't willing to do that, not even for a few hours. Sin's power was strong. Like a beguiling force, it tugged at you until it catapulted you, headfirst, into the cesspool.

Rita had definitely been no stranger to the struggle not to succumb to fleshly desires. Why, in the early months of her spiritual makeover, she had almost given in to sin's temptation to try her hand, once again, with the god of luck and wager—only a dollar—on the lottery. Thank God that when she'd stepped up to the window to place her bet, the machine had run out of paper. Being in a hurry, Rita couldn't afford to wait. She had attributed her failure to thwart the prodding of sin at its first insistence to not being fully convinced of the Lord's forgiveness for her previous lifestyle. After she had called her pastor for reassurance of God's forgiveness and confided her near-fatal temptation, her prayer sisters had rushed right over. They had prayed into the early hours of the morning.

Three months later, Rita found herself having to be reinvigorated once again when the curse words she swore she'd never use again had reintroduced themselves whenever someone cut her off in traffic or when the lines in the grocery store were too long and she was already late for church. And there had been one lonely Saturday night when she'd found herself at a nightclub on Green Road, slowly sipping a Long Island iced tea while a very young Richard Roundtree look-alike massaged her right thigh under the table and insisted they go back to his place, where it was much quieter, to get to know each other better.

It was then that Rita knew she'd have to do something drastic. She decided that she would talk about God every chance she got, and it worked. Soon her co-workers stopped asking her out for drinks after work, and she was more patient while driving or standing in line at the grocery store. She'd even gained new friends who shared her spiritual views, unlike Jaki, who talked only of partying and sexual exploits. Jaki was shameful, really. It sickened Rita, but she wouldn't judge Jaki. That was God's job. All Rita could do was help to point Jaki in the right direction and pray for her.

Rita wet a paper towel with cold water and wiped her forehead. How dare Jaki throw Rita's past in her face? If the Lord had seen fit to rid Rita of sin and eternally wash her clean by the water of baptism, who was Jaki to criticize her for bettering her life? Rita had labored long and hard for five years reinventing herself. She'd gone to the library and checked out audio materials on improving her speech, changed her vocabulary, and read self-help books on how to be a better person. Jaki would do well to heed her example.

Exiting the rest room, Rita cautiously looked both ways, not wanting her boss to see her. She glanced toward Mrs. Marbury's office and saw that she was on the phone, having what looked like a very intense conversation. She quickly half-walked, half-ran to her desk.

Blink, blink, blink . . .

The e-mail icon beckoned. *What now?* Rita wondered. It's probably Jaki apologizing for her ill-mannered behavior. Rita clicked on the icon, shaped like a small envelope, and waited for the apology to download. But it wasn't an apology from Jaki; it was that Michael person again.

Subject: Pager Number
From: "Michael Adams" <bcing@funmail.com>
Sent: Mon 2/5/07 07:15:34 A.M.
To: "Rita Collier" <R.Collier@Hemphilstores.com>

    I forgot that you don't have my pager number. Here it is, baby: 555-2341.

Peace, Mike

Did this man have no shame? Rita sighed. She was both distressed and relieved: distressed because this new e-mail forced her to have to reply to this man and tell him that he had the wrong person; relieved because now she would have an opportunity to help him and his girlfriend get saved.

Rita clicked on "Reply" and composed her message:

Subject: Re: Pager number
From: "Rita Collier"<R.Collier@Hemphilstores.com>
Sent: Mon 7/5/2007 7:35:34 A.M.
To: "Michael Adams" <boing@funmail.com>

Mr. Adams:

    As you can see by my e-mail address, you have directed your correspondence to me in error. For several reasons, I am quite sure that I am not your intended audience. One of which is that I did not spend an evening with you having a record-setting "lovemaking session." Another would be because I do not, as you say, have a "li'l freak" in me. Lastly, I assure you that I know of no such thing to do with my tongue that would elicit such a response as you have made. I am a Christian woman of the highest moral fiber and find such behavior repulsive. I might suggest that becoming acquainted with God might do you and your friend a world of good.

I would advise you to speak directly with your lady friend in order that you might secure the correct e-mail address.

Thank you,

R. Collier

After proofreading her reply twice, Rita huffed and clicked the "Send" icon. *There, that should be the end of him!*

Mrs. Marbury had volunteered Rita's services for the Return Credit Card division today. However, Rita would much rather be doing data entry or customer service—anything but this menial task that was beneath someone of her stature. But when she'd questioned her boss, she'd simply been told that it was urgent; the more hands the better. Well, Rita fretted, if it was so urgent, why wasn't Jaki assigned to do it?

Rita could imagine how the scene had gone. Mrs. Marbury had probably told Jaki that she wanted her to work in the RCC division today. And Jaki, ghetto as ever, had probably stood there with her hand on her hip, finger stuck in the boss's face, telling her what she didn't feel like doing. Any other employee would be fired for insubordination, but not Jaki. For some reason, Mrs. Marbury always let Jaki have things her way. Always perturbed by this show of favoritism, Rita would calm herself with the knowledge that she was being made a much better person by her long suffering endurance of slackers. Each day when Rita punched out, she had a clean conscience, having given her employer an honest day's work.

For the third time that morning, the familiar blinking of the e-mail icon distracted her. She clicked on the message:

Subject: Re: Re: Pager number
From: "Michael Adams" <boing@funmail.com>
Sent: Mon 2/5/07 7:41:22 A.M.
To: "Rita Collier" <R.Collier@Hemphilstores.com>

Ms. Collier,

Please accept my apology for misdirecting that message. As far as what you said about me getting to know God, thank you very much, but I do know God. You worship Him your way (and I promise I won't criticize you for that ☺) and I'll worship Him my way.

Peace, Mike

BTW, what country are you from?

Rita put the message in the suspend mode while she contemplated the postscript. What did he mean by that question? He was probably being sarcastic. His kind usually got that way after someone pointed out their shortcomings. She didn't know what kind of God he worshiped, but she was sure it wasn't the one in the Bible. It couldn't be; otherwise he would know that sex is a beautiful thing that should never be polluted, as he and his lady friend had obviously done by being freaky.

Rita tabbed to the Fastdata address search screen to search for the street address of a credit card that had come back with the "no such address" box checked. She found the mistake, corrected it, put it in the proper stack, tallied her statistics, and rubber-banded the stack. She grabbed another batch and started the routine all over.

When she completed that batch, she looked at her watch and saw that it was already five minutes past her break time. "Jaki—" she started to say, then remembered their falling out and quickly shut her mouth.

Rita was getting ready to pause all of her programs when she saw that the forgotten e-mail message she had left in the suspend mode was awaiting a command. She decided to answer it.

Subject: Re: Re: Re: Pager number
From: "Rita Collier" <R.Collier@Hemphilstores.com>
Sent: Mon., 2/5/07 9:35:02 A.M.
To: "Michael Adams" <boing@funmail.com>

Mr. Adams:

        To answer your question, I am from the U.S. It puzzles me why you would ask such an absurd thing.

R. Collier

Casting a condescending glance in Jaki's direction, Rita bounced off in the direction of the cafeteria.

Precisely fifteen minutes after she left, Rita was pushing her pocketbook back in the confines of her bottom drawer. A slip of paper displaying Mrs. Marbury's familiar round writing was taped on her keyboard. Rita just knew it had to be bad news, so she pushed the piece of paper aside, unread, and re-opened her programs.

Again the mailbox icon blinked. She had never gotten this much email before; this was a record-setting day.

Subject: You
From: "Michael Adams" <boing@funmail.com>
Sent: Mon. 2/5/07 09:36:01 A.M.
To: "Rita Collier"<R.Collier@Hemphilstores.com>

Ms. Collier,

My question was not absurd. Your phraseology reminded me of the way some of our overseas clients speak. Real uppity like.

Look, I know we got off on the wrong foot, but something tells me you're not a bad person. Misguided maybe, but not bad. So what do you say we start over? I'll go first.

Hi, I'm Michael Adams. I'm 32, dark skinned, 5'11" (muscular build), bald, single. I'm a software developer for a large computer company in North Olmsted, Ohio. When I'm not spending time with my six-year-old son, I like going to jazz concerts, shooting hoops, chillin' with the fellas, or just kicking back for a nice, quiet evening with that special someone.

Your turn,

Mike

Rita hit the alt and tab keys simultaneously, exiting the e-mail screen back to her work screen. She hadn't imagined this Mike person possessing social skills, let alone an appreciation for jazz music. She had conjured an image of him lazing around for the better part of the day and spending the other part in front of his computer screen wheedling away time better spent out looking for work. She was pleasantly surprised to be wrong, if she could believe what he had typed.

What did she care anyway? The fact remained that his initial e-mail showed he was not a man of good quality. While he was coming on to her, what of his lady friend? As Rita had suspected, this Mike person was a playboy.

Her initial thought that it was God's guidance that had steered him to her was now tinged with doubt. Could she be wrong? She thought of her favorite Bible verse, 1 Corinthians 15:33: "Be not deceived: evil communications corrupt good manners."No truer could those words be than in this situation. Still a thought nagged at Rita: As a Christian, it was her responsibility to help save every soul with which she came in contact. To help this Mike person would require her being conversational and genuinely concerned. Hadn't the apostle Paul said that he had become all things to everyone so that he might save some? If Rita was to help save this man's soul, as she now believed God had directed her to, she too would have to assume a role.

An hour later, after finishing another batch of returned credit cards, Rita opened the mail window once again to reply to the latest e-mail message.

Subject: Re: You
From: "Rita Collier"<R.Collier@Hemphilstores.com>
Sent: Mon 2/5/07 10:52:12 A.M.
To: "Michael Adams" <boing@funmail.com>

Mr. Adams:

Praise the Lord!

Thank you for expressing interest in wanting to get to know me. Be assured that I am flattered. I will tell you about myself—not because I am interested, mind you, but because

I feel it is the polite thing to do, seeing that you have shared your information with me.

Let me commend you on being an active parent in your child's life. I believe that the increase in violent crimes committed by children is the sad consequence of a lack of parental guidance, discipline, and quality time spent with one's children. Not to be forgotten is the need for spiritual guidance as well. Wouldn't you agree, Mr. Adams?

You said that you worked for a large computer company in North Olmsted, Ohio. What a coincidence that we are in close geographic proximity.

I do wonder, however, if you work for a computer company, why you have chosen to use a novelty e-mail address. Surely you cannot be hiding from the woman you spent the fabulous night of "love-making" with. I should hope that the two of you would be beyond such pretenses, especially since you have shared something as spiritual as a physical act of love. To be sure, that certainly is not my business.

As for personal information: My name is Rita Collier. I am 29, 5'3", light-skinned, slender, shoulder-length hair, single and childless. I am a credit specialist for a large department store chain (Hemphil department stores, as you know by my e-mail address). Like you, I am a connoisseur of jazz music, next to gospel music. Who, may I ask, is your favorite jazz performer? When I am not volunteering my time somewhere or spending time with family, I can usually be found attending whatever gospel play is currently on stage at the Cleveland Play House.

R. Collier

Waiting for a reply from Mr. Adams, Rita retrieved Mrs. Marbury's note from the corner of her desk. Mrs. Marbury wanted to know if Rita was available to work overtime. Rita closed her fist over the paper and threw it into the trash. As much as she hated doing the task she was conscripted to do, she thought a moment and decided that she could use the extra money. She contemplated answering yes but decided she would give Mrs. Marbury her answer after lunch, when she'd had more time to think about it.

Blink . . . blink . . . blink.

Subject: Satisfied?
From: "Michael Adams"
<Michael.Adams@Firstsystems.com>
Sent: Mon 2/5/07 11:15:33 A.M.
To: "Rita Collier" <R.Collier@Hemphilstores.com>

Rita (may I call you that? All this Mr. and Ms. is too formal),

I like to think of myself as a progressive male, always learning and improving who I am. Therefore, I have no need or desire to play games. I did not use my work e-mail system because the e-mail I was sending was not work-related.

I agree with you about today's children. I try to spend as much time with my son as I can, teaching him right from wrong. Every weekend that I have him, I make sure that we go to church. The weekends when he's with his mother are another story.

What religion are you, if you don't mind me asking? I'm Baptist.

From your description, you sound like you're pretty. So my question to you is, why are you single? You're intelligent, spiritual, no kids, and fine. Don't tell me you're one of those career women who want a brother to be making six figures before you'll give him some holla. Too many of the sistas are like that.

Ever been married?
Mike

Rita noticed that he had switched to his work e-mail. So he worked at First Systems, one of the largest software and technology developers in Northeast Ohio. She Googled the company and clicked on the link to the Web site, pointed her mouse to the company directory, and searched for Michael Adams. He had been telling the truth, at least about his job. She logged into her LinkedIn account and searched for his name. She found his name along with some very impressive credentials. He had graduated from the Massachusetts Institute of Technology cum laude with a bachelor's degree in computer science, then two years later graduated with a master's in software development and management. He was promoted to his current position six months ago, and now here he was wasting precious company time sending lewd e-mail messages to strangers. Besides that, he was getting way too personal with his questions. Her criterion for a soul mate was none of his business. He sure wasn't it. Rita wondered if he had his son every weekend and if that was the only time he went to church.

Mike had made a good point about not using his work e-mail for his personal correspondence. But what of using company time for non-work related things? She hoped he hadn't added that comment to try to show her up. Had it not been for her strong belief that God had directed Mike to her to help save Mike's soul, Rita would not have been using her work e-mail system or company time for personal business either.

Rita rolled her eyes at Mike's statement about money. That was all men ever thought about. Well, that and the other thing. She'd read a survey a while back that said that the average male spent eight of his waking hours thinking about sex. Another survey she had read said that the top three priorities for a man all began with the letter F: finances, fun . . ., and the other one too vulgar for Rita to even think the word.

Subject: Re: Satisfied?
From: "Rita Collier" <R.Collier@Hemphilstores.com>
Sent: Mon., 2/5/2007 11:23:01 A.M.
To: "Michael Adams"
<Michael.Adams@Firstsystems.com>

Mr. Adams,

No, I do not mind if you call me Rita. And no, I have never been married. I think it is commendable that you take your son to church. Some parents simply send their children to Sunday school while they sleep in.

I have to tell you that my being single has nothing to do with the man's financial status. Material things mean nothing to me. I believe a person should choose a mate based on his or her spiritual qualifications. By the way, I'm a born again Christian. Now let me ask you a question: have you accepted the Lord Jesus as your personal Savior?

Rita

That should keep the conversation on the right track, she thought. On her way out for lunch, Rita stopped by Mrs. Marbury's office to let her know that she would have an answer for her before the end of the day.

Rita peeked over into Jaki's cubicle on her return from lunch and saw that her computer was off. She must have left early. That was another thing that bothered Rita about Jaki—she was always leaving early or coming in late for one stupid reason or another.

"Hey, Rita, did you hear?" Georgia, whose hair was always in a perpetual state of confusion, wore a concerned expression. "Jaki's mother had a massive stroke."

"Oh!" Rita said, shocked. Thanks for telling me," she mumbled, ashamed that she had considered Jaki's early departure to be another frivolous squandering of time. When Georgia turned to leave, Rita dropped heavily into her chair, bowed her head, and offered up a silent prayer for the Morgan family.

Far from uneventful, like most days in the National Accounts Department, this day was turning out to be full of adventure.

Raising her head, Rita turned her attention to the computer screen.

Blink . . . blink . . . blink.

Subject: Salvation
From: "Michael Adams"
<Michael.Adams@Firstsystems.com>
Sent: Mon 2/5/2007 13:02:04 P.M.
To: "Rita Collier" <R.Collier@Hemphilstores.com>

        Yes, I have accepted Jesus as my personal Savior.

You mentioned in one of your messages something about sex being spiritual. It's interesting that you would equate the two. I sort of think of it as being that also, but in a different way. I see it as a vehicle that God created in order for men and women to be able to communicate on a deeper level. There are some things that words alone cannot express. And what better way to do it than with that perfect vehicle, the body? What are your thoughts on the subject, Rita?

Mike

Rita swallowed hard. She wanted to abort the conversation; however, she hadn't backed down from a God-given assignment yet, and she wouldn't back down now.

Subject: Re: Salvation
From: "Rita Collier" <R.Collier@Hemphilstores.com>
Sent: Mon., 2/5/2007 13:11:34 P.M.
To: "Michael Adams"
<Michael.Adams@Firstsystems.com>

Mike,

My thought on the subject of sex is that it should only be shared between two people who are wholly committed to each other in a relationship built on mutual love and trust, in marriage, which is what God requires. Are you and your lady friend in that sort of relationship?

Rita

Oh my God! Why did I ask that? I don't want him to think I'm interested in him. If only I could call back the e-mail and erase it.

Rita tabbed back to her work screen; she had two more batches to complete before her shift ended. She rubber-banded the batch she had just completed and reached for another. When she came back from her break, she would have an hour and fifteen minutes left on her shift.

In the break room, she found it hard to concentrate on the newspaper in front of her. Why had she added that last part to the e-mail? She worried her brow into a furrow, her chin resting in her cupped palms. Was it perhaps that she had been single so long that she secretly desired this man? No, that made no sense. He wasn't the first man to express interest in her. Was it the mysteriousness of it all? He was an interesting man, a thinking man, someone who wasn't put off by her proper speech and exceptional observations.

Returning to her desk, Rita tapped the mouse and her monitor sprang to life. The mailbox icon in the corner of the screen flashed.

Subject: Let's meet
From: "Michael Adams"
<Michael.Adams@Firstsystems.com>
Sent: Mon 2/5/2007 14:17:43 P.M.
To: "Rita Collier" <R.Collier@Hemphilstores.com>

Rita,
           It's two o'clock and we've been e-mailing back and forth all day. I don't know about you, but I didn't get much work done today ☺. I've really enjoyed talking to you. Let's meet after work. I get off at 3:00. We could grab something to eat at a restaurant with lots of people around. That way, you'll feel safe. You can never be too careful nowadays. I'll answer your questions about what sort of relationship

me and my lady friend have, and you can tell me all about my heathen ways. Deal?

Mike

P.S. I feel as though God directed me to you, Rita.

Rita blinked once and closed her eyes tight, confused. Was Mike being facetious? She couldn't believe that he shared her opinion about their encounter. *Is this you, God?* she silently questioned. That ol' snake Lucifer could be a sneaky devil, making himself into an angel of light, pretending to be good and pure when really it was evil he sought. Rita prayed for God's direction. She needed a sign, a word, a look, a sound—something that would allow her to know if indeed this was divine direction. She prayed fervently and rapidly, her words colliding together so that they became words only God could understand.

Rita's head began to ache. What to do? This man was a stranger; some man she knew only from words typed onto a computer screen. For all she knew he could be a rapist, a serial killer, anything. Rita decided that she wouldn't answer him; she'd continue with the conversation as though he hadn't asked her to meet with him.

Subject: Re: Let's meet
From: "Rita Collier" <R.Collier@Hemphilstores.com>
Sent: Mon 2/5/2007 14:29:16 P.M.
To: "Michael Adams"
<Michael.Adams@Firstsystems.com>

Mike,

Yes, I am aware that we've been communicating for the better part of this day. Unlike you, I managed to do quite a bit of work. I apologize for the distraction. It has been quite interesting hearing your views and getting to know a little of your life. If it's not too much of an imposition, tell me, how long have you been saved?

Rita

Rita jumped slightly at the sound of Mrs. Marbury's voice behind her.

"Rita, what have you decided about the overtime?" Rita detected annoyance in the massive, imposing woman's voice and didn't know if it was because she'd been standing there long enough to read what Rita had written or if this was just her usual annoyance.

"I'm sorry, Mrs. Marbury, it completely slipped my mind. No, I'm not available to work extra hours tonight. If the offer is good for tomorrow night, I'd be more than happy to stay a few extra hours."

"Not tomorrow. Wednesday?"

"Wednesdays are my prayer meeting nights. I couldn't possibly stay— sorry. What about Jaki?" Rita asked and instantly regretted it when she saw the look on her boss's face. She'd forgotten that Jaki's mother was lying in the hospital, probably on the verge of death, and here Rita was worrying about whether Jaki could take up the slack and work a few extra hours. What a fine Christian attitude that was.

After it was established that she would work three extra hours on Thursday and Friday, Rita rested her chin on her fist and stared at the blinking mailbox icon. The pace of her heart quickened in anticipation of reading Mike's reply. *What did he say?* she wondered. Would he try to pressure her to meet with him, or had he gone along with her game of make-believe? Rita swallowed hard before opening the e-mail.

Subject: Re: Re: Let's meet
From: "Michael Adams"
<Michael.Adams@Firstsystems.com>
Sent: Mon 2/5/07 14:33:48 P.M.
To: "Rita Collier" <R.Collier@Hemphilstores.com>

I've been saved for three years.

Mike

That was it? Rita stared, dumbfounded, at the screen. No pressure, no declarations of how he'd behave like a perfect gentleman if they met? Nothing? What was she supposed to do now? How should she respond? Was she even supposed to? Rita didn't know whether she should be relieved or annoyed. After all, this was the perfect out, and she should take it. Mike couldn't possibly expect her to reply after a response like that, could he? On deeper reflection, Rita felt cheated. They had communicated all day, and now it would end like this. No fuss, quick and painless. Well, if that was how he wanted it, then she would leave it at that. Let him wonder why she hadn't replied.

Just then the phone on Rita's desk chirped. "Hemphil Department Store, Return Credit Card division. This is Rita, how may I help you?"

"Rita, hi. This is Mike."

The voice on the other end was cheerful and upbeat. "Mike who?" Rita asked. Not e-mail Mike, surely.

"The Mike you've been e-mailing all day," he said, laughing. His laughter was infectious, and Rita caught herself smiling. A familiar tingle went through Rita. The temptation was too great. *Dear Lord Jesus,* help me! Mike had gone to the trouble of tracking her down, and Rita didn't know if she should be flattered or afraid. Suddenly she felt fearful. Why hadn't she immediately been suspicious that this man whom she only knew by a few keystrokes on a computer screen had gone through the trouble to locate her?

"Hello? Are you still there?" Mike asked.

"Yes, yes, I'm still here. Listen, Mike, how did you find me?" she asked, her voice wavering slightly. The division she worked in didn't list support staff or their direct-dial phone numbers on the Web site directory.

"I called your human resources department and was transferred to your supervisor, who transferred the call to you."

Rita was taken aback at how matter-of-factly he said it—as if he did this sort of thing every day, no big deal. Well, it was a big deal to Rita. She didn't appreciate it, and she told him as much.

"I'm sorry," Mike said. "If I knew you'd trip, I would have let it rest. But I thought that since you seemed so concerned about my spiritual welfare, and you didn't answer my question about getting together after work, I'd give you a call and reassure you that I was on the up. But since it seems that you're uninterested and not as concerned as I thought, I'll let you get back to your work. Have a nice day, Ms. Collier."His words were clipped, and Rita detected regret in his tone.

"No, wait! I apologize if I hurt your feelings. But I have a right to be suspicious of strange men who call my place of employment uninvited. Let's be realistic, Mike. I don't know you, and you don't know me. For all we know of each other, neither of us could be what we profess." Her words sounded braver than she felt.

"You're right," Mike conceded. "I apologize for being so forward. It's just that your e-mails sounded so urgent. I like that. I mean, you don't find many people who genuinely seem to care about other people's spiritual well-being .Don't get me wrong, I'm not looking to be saved, because I already am. It's just your concern touched something in me, that's all. Anyway, I'll let you get back to work. Maybe someday, if it's God's will, we'll meet face-to-face."

There he went again, talking about God's will. The confusion that Rita had felt earlier about this whole encounter returned. She wanted to keep him talking to find out whether he was for real. The rhythmic way the words rolled off his tongue put Rita at ease, and she felt her armor loosening.

"You believe, do you, that God is responsible for us becoming aware of each other?" Rita asked.

"Yeah, I do. How would you explain the misdirected e-mail?"

Rita thought for a moment, unable to come up with a counterargument.

"Exactly!" Mike said. "Listen, it's already 2:45. Fifteen more minutes and I'm off the clock. Look, Rita, I know this is a strange situation, and normally I don't do this sort of thing, but I'd really like to meet you after work. Just to talk. You can bring the whole office with you if that'll make you feel safer. What do you say?"

She could always say no. If she did, though, she might be denying God's opportunity to work through her to lead this lost soul back onto the right path. It was clear by his first e-mail that he had strayed and needed readjusting. What was there to fear? Either she believed this was God's will or she didn't. If she believed, then God would protect her from harm.

That all sounded simple enough, but there was another problem: what if this Mike looked as good as he sounded? Rita didn't need the temptation. She had walked the straight and narrow consistently for four years. There was no room for backsliding now, or ever. God would protect her from that temptation also, she decided.

"All right, Michael," Rita heard herself say. "I'll meet you at the Macaroni Grill out by Great Northern Mall at four o'clock." Rita thought she heard Mike let out a sigh of relief. She couldn't be sure because her heart was pounding loudly in her ears.

After exchanging identifying information with Mike, Rita called the florist and had flowers sent to the hospital for Jaki's mother. Then she put in a call to her mother to let her know where she would be and with whom, just in case.

Pulling into the parking lot of the Macaroni Grill, Rita spotted a gold Ford Expedition, the color, make, and model that Mike said he drove. She parked, then checked her face in the mirror, freshened her lipstick, and ran a finger across her eyebrows. Stepping into the restaurant, Rita scanned the room for a tall black man wearing a tan pullover sweater with a pair of khaki pants. The hostess approached, asking Rita how many were in her party. Rita was about to answer when she spotted a man fitting Mike's description sitting in a booth, looking casually in her direction.

"The man sitting in that booth," Rita said, pointing in the man's direction, "is he here by himself?"

The hostess gave Rita a once-over and said almost territorially, "He's waiting for someone."

"I see," Rita said, fidgeting nervously with the belt of her black wool pea coat. "Uh . . . I don't want to impose upon you, but may I ask you to find out who he's waiting for?"

"Come again?" the hostess said, screwing up her face.

"You see, I'm meeting someone here . . . well . . . I'm not sure what he looks like. Please, Miss, will you ask him?"

The hostess's expression softened slightly, and she went to ask. "Someone named Rita," the hostess replied when she'd returned.

"Oh," Rita breathed.

"Sorry, Miss," the hostess said, flushing a reddish pink. She seemed genuinely sorry for Rita.

"No, no," Rita reassured. "I'm Rita. I just didn't expect him to . . . well, I don't know what I expected." Rita thanked the hostess as she led her to the booth where Mike sat waiting.

The man who stood to greet her had unnervingly good looks. The bridge of his nose had a small hump, giving character to an otherwise flawless face. Not many men could pull off the bald look, but Mike's baldness seemed custom-made, to the point that it was hard to imagine this man ever having hair. His smooth, dark skin was without blemish, and the clothes that hid his nakedness seemed like intruders. Mike proffered his hand to Rita; his nails were clean, she noticed, and his hands were soft too. That was a plus. Mike waited for Rita to sit before seating himself. *Too good to be true.*

"So I finally get to put a face to those stinging words and that sultry voice." Mike smiled.

"My words can't have been all that bad; otherwise we wouldn't be sitting here." Rita attempted a smile, but she knew it probably looked more like a sneer; she could feel the nervousness pulling her face to one side.

"Your words did sort of cut, but I'm not saying that's necessarily a bad thing. It's good to know you're not shy about saying what's on your mind."

Before Rita could reply, Mike abruptly changed the conversation. "So, Miss Collier, do you need to look at the menu, or do you already know what you want?"

Rita scanned the menu, and when the server arrived at their table, they placed their orders. Conversation flowed easily. They talked of childhoods growing up in impoverished areas of the inner city of Cleveland, Ohio, Rita in the King Kennedy housing projects and Mike in the Longwood Estates. Mike was a late-in-life baby, and Rita was the illegitimate child of a sixteen-year-old. Rita had four siblings, of whom she was the oldest; Mike was the youngest of five. Mike especially liked the Rippertons and James Cleveland, while Rita enjoyed listening to Shirley Caesar and Grover Washington, Jr., and they both regretted that he died so young.

Mike told Rita a little about his son, Cody, and the relationship he had with his ex. Rita found herself opening up to Mike about areas of her life she had wanted to leave far behind. Something in his spirit settled her and made her feel comfortable. When she learned that Mike's father was the assistant pastor of a well-known Baptist church in the inner city that broadcast its Sunday services on the radio, she understood what that something was. Apparently, Mike had watched his father co-shepherd the congregation and had learned his manner well. This impressed her more than him volunteering his time and services at several east side nursing facilities, teaching the elderly how to use computers and particularly e-mail so that they could keep in touch with family and friends.

Mike's infectious laughter made Rita laugh as he related a funny story about one of the nursing facility residents, Mr. Abernathy, being caught viewing pornography. Rita hadn't wanted to laugh; normally she wouldn't have. Maybe it was the atmosphere, or being in the company of this compassionate man, or nervousness. She still wasn't totally convinced that this was God's doing.

Mike folded his arms across his chest and pressed his back against the seat. He assessed Rita before he spoke. "So, Miss Rita Collier, do I pass the test?"

"What test?" Rita asked curiously.

"You know, the crazy test? What have you decided—am I some lunatic perpetrator, or am I just as sane as you? You are sane, aren't you?" Mike asked playfully, a mischievous smile sliding across his lips. He rested the back of his head in the palms of his hands.

Rita's eyes lingered too long on Mike's, and she felt an urge to reach out and touch him. She coughed away her embarrassment. What was taking the server so long in bringing their desserts? Rita wondered. Mike's raised eyebrows told Rita that he was expecting an answer.

"I certainly don't think you're crazy, Mike. To the contrary, actually. As a matter of fact, I think you're a fascinating man, if all you say is true." Rita didn't know what it would take, short of the Lord speaking directly to her, to convince her that Mike was legitimate.

"I see you're a tough audience, Rita. I can't convince you that I am who I say I am, and you won't let yourself be convinced. So what now?"

Just then the server arrived with dessert and a fresh pot of coffee.

Rita sipped the hot liquid and thought a moment. She didn't want the evening to end just yet. She hoped nothing in her manner betrayed her feelings. "What would you like to happen?" *Loaded question! Never ask a man what he wants. It all comes down to one thing.*

If Mike's mind was on impure thoughts, nothing in his words or actions gave it away. Instead he looked thoughtful and then said, "Tell me about your work."

Shocked and relieved, Rita pushed away from the table, picked imaginary fuzz from her navy blue slacks, and told Mike all about her work and some of her co-workers.

"One co-worker, who's also a friend, has me concerned," she confided.

"Concerned why?"

"For one, she doesn't believe in God. Oh, she says she does, but she hasn't set foot inside of a church in more than twenty years. We used to party together, when I did that sort of thing."

Mike nodded thoughtfully.

"I've tried to help her, but you know the type." Rita knew Mike would understand, having been raised by a man of the cloth and himself being saved.

"What type is that?"

Rita looked perplexed. "You know, the loose type. She would rather worship herself and the men she beds than worship the Lord Jesus. She keeps company with riffraff and lowlifes. She needs to go to church so she can meet a decent man, someone she can settle down with, and get her life in order. If it weren't for knowing me, she wouldn't know any good, decent Christians. Every time I invite her to my church, she always has an excuse." Rita leaned in as though sharing a secret and said in a lowered tone, "If I were to ask her to go out to a nightclub on a Saturday night, she'd make time for that. But let me ask her to go praise the Lord, and she suddenly has a million and one things to do. You know, *that* type."

"Oh. Yeah. *That* type. I know what you mean." Mike's expression had changed, and his voice had lost some of its congeniality. "So why do you stay friends with her if she's so bad?"

It was a fair question, so why did it sound like an accusation? "I suppose It's out of pity. No, let me rephrase that. It's because we've been through a lot together, and I feel I owe it to her to try to help her find her way back to God."

"Maybe she's searching for God and she just didn't feel it necessary to fill you in on that."

Rita snorted. "Right! Believe me, I'm the first person she'd tell. She wouldn't be able to resist rubbing it in my face. She's that sort of person, trust me. I've known Jaki for ten years." Rita stopped suddenly, realizing that they had spent an enormous amount of time talking about Jaki. "Are you always this interested in other people's lives, or do you have an ulterior motive?" Rita smiled when she asked the question.

"You seemed to need to tell me about your co-worker, and no I don't have an ulterior motive," Mike said.

The server approached and asked if she could get anything else for them, and when they both said no, she placed the check holder in front of Mike, who picked it up and pulled out his wallet. Placing his credit card in the holder, he cleared his throat. He seemed nervous for some reason.

Okay, here it comes. He's going to tell me that he's some sort of weirdo freak or something.

"I have a confession to make, Rita," he said, his brown eyes holding her gaze. "That e-mail that I sent you this morning was no mistake. A mutual friend gave me your e-mail address and encouraged me to contact you. The only things our friend told me about you is that you are a beautiful, spiritual person who loves jazz and is heavily into your religion. You sounded like the sort of person I've been looking for, so I said a prayer to God and decided to approach you the way I did because I wanted to see if you walked the walk. At first it seemed like we might have something. I mean, it's obvious that spiritual things are important to you. And we have a few things in common. But after hearing you run down your coworker who's supposed to also be a good friend for the last twenty minutes, I've got to wonder if you even know what it means to be a Christian."

All the color drained out of Rita's face, and her jaw went slack. She was truly speechless.

Mike, however, seemed to have just gotten started. "At first I thought you had the misguided zeal of a newly converted person. But you," Mike shook his head. "You're another story altogether. You're mean-spirited and judgmental. You got this whole holier-than-thou complex going on, and anyone who doesn't believe what you believe, *how* you believe it, is going to hell."

The server brought the receipt for Mike to sign and, smiling, told the couple to enjoy their night. Mike signed the receipt, pocketed his credit card, and looked with regret at Rita's ashen face.

Rita found her voice and asked nervously, "Who put you up to this?"

"Nobody put me up to this, but Jaki Morgan gave me your e-mail address, because she thought that we were right for each other. She was wrong."

A knot formed in Rita's throat, and she felt a dark cloud descend upon her spirit, overshadowing her short-lived joy. That very moment, sitting in the Macaroni Grill on Great Northern Boulevard at 6:45 p.m. on Monday, February 5, 2007, Rita Collier was humbled.

TRANSITIONS

"CLEANUP ON AISLE SEVEN. . . . CUSTOMER SERVICE manager to register twelve." Day in and day out, I have to hear the blare of the loudspeakers as commands are called into the store's PA system, until my eardrums nearly collapse. Between the crackle and pop of the loudspeaker, the thudding noise the electronic doors make when they slam shut, and the mind-melting humidity, I'm about to lose my mind up in here. I think about the lyrics of that old DMX jam, "Up in Here," as I plaster a fake smile on my face and greet a customer who should have spent about five more minutes caring for his personal hygiene.

I've been working at this godforsaken QualMart store for too long. First off, the store is in a bad neighborhood, but lately it's been getting worse. A few months ago, the bank next door got robbed for the third time in two years. Half the time the heating and cooling systems don't work, and the store is dreary looking all the time, especially since Mr. Hall, the owner, decided to install motion sensor lights to conserve energy. Most of the time, we can't tell if the lights don't work or if the bulbs are blown. The motion sensor lights were a good idea, but he could have at least installed higher voltages. The other day I almost tripped over two teenagers making out in the pet food aisle. The lights are nothing compared to the smell. I think they must have built this store on top of a garbage dump, because when the wind blows up from the north, it takes everything in me not to gag.

Most days I like my job. It's just that standing on my feet all day, listening to customers complain about how much money they don't make and how boring their jobs are gets on my nerves. Between the complaining and the crazy conversations I have with the customers, this job can sometimes be pretty entertaining.

The other day this tall, Amazon-like creature who looked to be at least a hundred years old comes up to my register and asks me if we sell lacy nighties. I told her yeah and pointed her to the aisle. A few minutes later she comes back to my register complaining that we don't have her size. Excuse me, but what does a hundred-year-old Amazon intend to do with a lace nightie anyway? I asked her and was shocked at her answer. She said she'd met a man on the Internet and that night they were planning to meet in person for the first time. She wanted to "be prepared just in case he turned out to be a cutie." Yuck! And they're supposed to be our role models? I don't think so! If I'd had her for a grandmother, I'd probably have more than the three kids I already have.

Let me tell you, being a single parent is not easy! It wouldn't be so bad if all my kids had the same daddy, but they don't and I can't change that. I had Jarrod (my oldest son, he's six) when I was eighteen. He was my graduation present. Some present! Don't get me wrong; I love all of my kids. But when I was in high school, I had dreams—big dreams!

My plans were to go to culinary school, someday own my own catering business, marry my high school sweetheart Reggie Clark, and have five children. Even if I couldn't accomplish all my goals, I *definitely* wanted to marry Reggie! Reggie had broad linebacker shoulders (he was an outside linebacker for the Rhodes High School Rams in Cleveland) and huge hands. I used to love for him to grab me around my waist when we walked side by side; it made me feel secure. Reggie was the cutest guy I had ever known. He had pretty, bronze skin and wavy, sandy brown hair that he used to wear tied back in a ponytail. I loved stroking the fine hairs of his sideburns and his thin beard whenever he kissed me with those baby-soft lips. And when he looked at me with his big, round, hazel-colored eyes, I thought I would float up to heaven. Reggie Clark was the love of my life for three long, beautiful years. He was absolutely perfect. As far as I was concerned, Reggie walked on water. I know my dreams for my future sound country, but those were my dreams. Unfortunately, the only part of my plan that came true was that I did have Reggie's baby. A month before graduation, I found out I was pregnant. I really believed Reggie would stick by me. Boy, was I wrong. He ran like Carl Lewis doing the 400-meter relay.

Jarrod hears from his dad twice a year: his birthday and Christmas. That's cool. At least he keeps in touch, unlike Shania's daddy—she's my second child. I met Shania's father, Nate Jefferson, when I was working at a fast-food restaurant; he was my supervisor. When I saw that smooth ebony skin; those pretty green eyes with long, curly lashes; and his body, built like a Greek god, I was hypnotized. I thought he was the most exotic-looking man I had ever seen. He was half Irish and half Indo-Trinidadian.

Nate's body was cut in all the right places: washboard abs, bulging biceps and triceps, and rock-hard, toned calves. For a guy as cute as he was, he was nice too. Usually cute guys are conceited and into themselves. Not Nate. He used to always ask me about Jarrod and make sure that I had enough money to buy diapers and food for my baby, and he would even make sure that I got first dibs on overtime so that I could have a little extra cheddar for whatever. And Nate used to hook me up with all the free food I wanted. But after a while, even free fast food gets tired. Just like Nate.

After we went out for a few months, Nate started to get possessive and jealous. He didn't want me spending time with my family and friends, and that caused a lot of friction in our relationship. Behind closed doors, he was mean and belligerent and verbally abusive. One Saturday night, my cousin Sunny was hanging out with me at my apartment, and Nate came home drunk at around 1:00 in the morning and started screaming and ranting like he was possessed or something.

***

Sunny and I had the volume on the CD player low so that we wouldn't wake the kids. We had just finished singing backup to Beyoncé's "Crazy in Love" track from her *Dangerously in Love* CD, giggling like teenagers, when we heard a key turn in the lock. Sunny looked like she wanted to jump out of her skin. She didn't know that I had given Nate a key to my apartment and that he was temporarily living with me.

Nate took one look at Sunny and flipped out. "Get out my house!" he screamed, his speech slurring.

Sunny and Nate did not get along. He disliked—no, hated—her because she was always calling him a loser and telling me that I needed to cut him loose. My cousin Sunny was not someone who cared what other people thought of her, so she said how she felt about whatever or whomever right to the person's face. Nate was no exception. I hadn't told Sunny about the "real" Nate because I knew that she would go blab it to my parents. They would think I was a failure, and I really wanted to show them that I could make my own way in this world. The truth is, I was barely scraping by and needed the extra money that Nate living with me provided. Besides, he was my baby's father.

"What you mean your house?" Sunny shot back. "You don't pay no rent up in here!"

"You don't know what I pay up in here!" Nate retorted. "I want you out of my house, now! Kick rocks! Be gone!" Nate picked up a plastic vase from the table and threw it at Sunny, narrowly missing her head.

Sunny rushed toward Nate and swiped at his face with her long nails, but he managed to stumble backwards just in time to miss having his eyes clawed out. The two of them were screaming and cussing at each other so loudly that I just knew the whole neighborhood would hear. I was more scared than I'd ever been.

"Please, y'all, don't get into this now. The kids are asleep, and I don't want the neighbors calling the police." I really only said the part about the neighbors for Sunny's benefit. Since Nate had been living with me, the neighbors had called the police four times because of our loud arguments. Nate had never hit me, but there were times when he came close. The wild, crazy look on his face and the two veins that bulged at his temples had me thinking that he was coming dangerously close to crossing that line right now. "Sunny, just leave," I said. "Okay?" I was desperate for her to leave, and it showed in the shaky tone of my voice. Sunny recognized it and squinted at me with suspicion. She didn't say anything, which was surprising; she just picked up her purse and car keys and went to the door. She threw a warning look at Nate before slamming the door behind her.

The loud noise woke the kids, and both Jarrod and Shania starting crying at the same time. The kids' crying must've distracted Nate, because he was no longer in a fighting mood. He stumbled to the bedroom, flopped down on the bed, and fell asleep with his clothes on. I stayed in the kids' room that night and thought about how I was going to get myself out of this mess.

Sunny, with her big mouth, told her mother what had happened, and her mother told my parents. My daddy was so bent he was ready to whip some Nate tail, but instead he and my mom said that me and the kids could come live at home for a while. I didn't know how bad off I was, living in that environment, until after being home for a bit I found myself screaming regularly at Jarrod for no reason. My mom caught me screaming at him a few times. One Sunday, after a real bad episode, she sat me down and we had a heart-to-heart about raising kids.

My mom's opinion means the world to me, and I didn't want her to think that I was a bad parent, so when she brought me some reading material she had borrowed from a friend of hers on escaping abusive relationships, I accepted it. At first I didn't read it because I didn't think it applied to me. But out of boredom one day, I picked it up and looked at some of it. As I read, I could see the picture of my situation coming into focus, and I knew that I had to address the issue or I would be setting up my son to be verbally abusive just like Nate. So I went to the library and found a whole bunch of books on raising kids and anger management like my mom's friend told me to, and I read all of them. Whenever I think of Nate, I want to scream. If it wasn't for his looks and his awesome body, Nate Jefferson would be a useless lump of flesh taking up precious space.

In the beginning after Nate and I broke up, my heart would ache for my daughter because her father had turned his back on her, but now I don't worry any more, for either of my children. As far as they are concerned, Howard Coleman is their daddy.

***

I met Howard when my daughter was six weeks old. I was leaving the clinic after having my six-week checkup when Howard approached me. He had on blue hospital scrubs, so I kinda figured he worked at the hospital. I was struggling with Jarrod, who was two at the time, and Shania was hollering up a storm.

"Going my way?" Howard had asked, gesturing for me to sit in the wheelchair he was pushing. I sat, grateful for the assistance, and Jarrod tried to join Shania on my lap. After Howard and I exchanged introductions, I learned that he was a pediatric RN in the Neonatal Intensive Care Unit (NICU). I remember thinking, *A male nurse. Must be gay!*

I sized Howard up as he unlocked the wheels of the chair. Definitely not my type. He was too dark, his features were too strong, and he was too squishy looking.

"Why don't you help me push the chair, little man?" Howard said to Jarrod. Jarrod looked over at me, and I nodded my head that it was okay. My son, who's normally shy, was talkative that day. He and Howard hit it off like long lost friends. Jarrod bombarded Howard with questions about his favorite subject: trucks. When Howard told Jarrod that he had a big black truck, Jarrod turned to me, excited that he was going to ride in a truck.

"No, Jarrod, we're not going to ride in his truck. He was just telling you that he has a truck," I explained to Jarrod, whose chin had begun to quiver.

"Hey," Howard said to Jarrod. We stopped moving forward and Howard put the brakes on the chair and stooped to Jarrod's height. "It's all good, little dude," he said. Howard's soft voice seemed to calm Jarrod, and it was having some sort of medicinal effect on me as well. The nervous, jittery feeling that had been with me for so long seemed to melt away.

"I got something better than a truck ride for you," Howard said, pulling a chain with keys and trinkets on it from his pocket. Howard took a trinket of a Mercedes SUV off the chain and handed it to Jarrod.

"No!" I told Howard. "You don't have to do that, really. He'll be okay. He has trucks at home." To Jarrod I said, "Give him back the truck, okay? And tell him thank you."

Jarrod pursed his lips, gripped the trinket tight in his little fist, and gave me a look of defiance that I had never seen him display. Just then he reminded me of his father, and before I knew what was happening, I had snatched him by the collar of his shirt and pulled him to me. "If you don't give Howard back his truck, he's going to see you get a butt whupping," I threatened. Jarrod whimpered and sniffed as if he was going to cry, but otherwise my words didn't seem to faze him.

"Whoa!" Howard said, holding his hands palms out to me. "It's all right. I don't mind. It's just a little toy. I can get another one for free."

I told Howard that I admired the way he came to Jarrod's defense, but my son had to learn that when I told him to do something, I was not going to tolerate any attitude from him.

"I understand what you're saying and I'm not trying to interfere with the way you discipline your son. All I'm saying is that it's not a big deal. I have a friend who works at a Mercedes dealership and they give those things out like candy."

He was so calm and cool when he spoke that I found it hard to take issue with anything he said. So I released Jarrod's shirt and told him I was sorry. I felt foolish because of the way I had handled things. I had been working hard on not being so impatient with Jarrod, and I thought I was doing well—until a few minutes ago. It's just that I had allowed myself to get my hopes up about Shania's father sticking around, and like Jarrod's father, he had disappeared without a trace.

I was living at home with my parents and they helped me when they could, but I couldn't keep depending on them. They had their own bills and whatnot. I was working at a dead-end office job, which wasn't my gig at all. Before I realized it, I was laying all of that on Howard, and he was taking it all in like I was sharing top secret information.

Howard had resumed pushing me in the wheelchair. As we got near to the exit, I was preparing myself to get out of the chair and walk the rest of the way to my car. Howard went right through the doors.

"What are you doing?" I said, twisting in the chair and looking at Howard suspiciously.

"I'm taking you to your car," he said, as if I was short-school-bus special. "Where are you parked?"

I pointed toward my car. "You don't have to do that. I'm good. I'm sorry I got heavy on you. I didn't mean to give you my life history. It's just that . . . well, I don't know what it is. But I appreciate you helping me out and giving my son a toy. I'm sure you've got to get back to work." I was stammering and tripping all over my words and I didn't know why. He was making me nervous, or maybe I was still embarrassed. Whatever it was, I just wanted to be gone.

"It's no problem," Howard said as he pushed me in the direction of my pointing. "You should hear some of the stories I hear working in the NICU. I guarantee, your life story is a cakewalk in comparison."

I'm sure he had a point, but I didn't appreciate him trivializing what I had been through and was going through. It was as if he had read my mind, because the next words out of his mouth were, "I'm not trying belittle what you've been through. I apologize if it sounded that way. It's just that the tragedy some of those babies suffer before they come through the NICU is crazy." We talked some more and Howard told me about some of the babies in his unit, and I felt myself getting curious about this man to whom I was not at all physically attracted.

By the time we reached my car, we had exchanged phone numbers and I had learned that he was single with no children, was twenty-six years old, lived alone, had three sisters and a brother, and had been a pediatric RN for three years.

That was almost four years ago. At first I was a little nervous about going out with Howard, because he was twenty-six and I was twenty. I know six years isn't a huge gap, but all the guys I'd ever dated were only a year or two older than me. Besides the age difference, Howard wasn't really my type. What caught my attention about him initially was that he's tall, the way I like my men. But other than that, he's too dark, his eyes are a little too far apart, his body is a tad flabby and soft in places where I like rock hard and solid, he's bald (by choice), and his face is clean-shaven. I was so messed up from previous relationships that I almost let those differences cause me to miss out on a blessing.

***

Howard and I had been going out for almost a year. I had recently turned twenty-one, and for some reason, I don't know why, I started to feel trapped. Things were going too perfectly; it all seemed too good to be true. I'd quit my desk job and went to work at an auto parts store, where the pay was a little better. I finally felt ready to take a stab at moving out on my own again, so I started looking for an apartment. Between my new pay and what Howard was giving me, I had enough to rent a one-bedroom apartment on the lower west side of Cleveland. Even though I was psyched about the idea of being on my own again, I couldn't shake that feeling of doom. I remember waking up every day feeling like tragedy was just around the corner.

I had made an appointment with a landlord to check out an apartment on Clark Avenue, and I was waiting for my cousin Sunny to pick me up when my cell rang. I knew it was Howard by the ringtone. I answered feeling cheery and upbeat, but when I told him where I was going, his reaction killed my buzz.

"Why would you want to live over there in that bad element?" he said.

"What's that supposed to mean?" I shot back.

"All I'm saying, Tam, is that you're better than that. I've seen the type of people that areas like that breed, and you're above that."

It wasn't so much his words as his attitude that had cut me. I told myself that I shouldn't be hurt or shocked, but the truth is, I was in love with Howard, only he didn't know it. When I met Howard, I had just moved back home. Although he knew about my situation living with Nate, we had never talked about where I was living. He didn't know that I was living on West 10th Street at the time.

"You think just because you grew up in Shaker Heights, you're better than people who live in low-income areas. And just what type of people does living in an area like Clark Avenue 'breed'?" I could feel myself working up to something, and I was ready to explode. I hated that judgmental type of attitude.

"Whoa, Tam," Howard said as if I were livestock that needed taming. "You're taking this way too seriously. All I meant is areas like that tend to breed a welfare-type mentality—always looking for a handout. There're generations of families living down there who seem to think the world owes them a living. Dudes go from one woman to the next like dogs, impregnating almost every female they lay with. Women got three, four, five kids and all of them have different daddies. Working in that area, I see this stuff every day. Before I transferred to the NICU, I was in the family medicine clinic. Some of those women came through the clinic almost every year, and each time a different father's name went on the forms they filled out." Howard stopped talking, and that feeling of doom that I had felt earlier had returned. It was like a ball of lead in the pit of my stomach.

Even though I was sure that I loved Howard, I was unsure of his feelings for me. Rather, I should say, I was unsure how he would feel about me when I told him that I had lived among that element that he was so dead set against. I was only twenty-one, but I felt a lot older. Ancient. Weary, my mom would call it. Really, I was just tired. Tired of always making the same stupid mistakes. Thinking that every guy I met was "the one." Thinking that I wouldn't be judged by the choices I made. And probably what hurt me most was thinking that any man would be cool with raising not one but two children who weren't biologically his. If my kids' own fathers didn't want them or love them enough to be present in their lives, then why would another man who had no blood ties feel any different?

Some of the initial fight that I had felt had gone out of me, but not so much that I couldn't give Howard attitude when I dropped my bomb on him.

"Yeah, well, you think you know so much, Mr. I-Got-a-College-Education. For your information, I used to live on West 10th Street right before I met you. And in case you forgot, I have two kids and they have different fathers! So I guess I ain't no different than those women with the 'welfare-type mentality' who live in those areas that breed those types of people." I could tell that my words had hit him hard because all I could hear on the line was dead silence. It was almost too quiet. I was beginning to think that Howard had hung up on me when he said, "Baby, I'm sorry. I didn't know. I didn't mean to make you feel . . ." His voice cracked and he cleared his throat. "I'm sorry, Tam," Howard whispered hoarsely. "All I mean is you're different from them. You got drive; you want something out of life."

I let the words hang in the air. I was disappointed. When you're in my situation (young, kids with different daddies), most people think that you came from the projects or your parents set a bad example. That's not my situation at all. My parents both went to college and have respectable jobs. My father is an investment broker, and my mother is a registered nurse. Howard knows that. Maybe the fact that we're not living in the projects is what blinded Howard to the fact that I'm really no different than those women he was dissing.

After that exchange, things between us cooled a little. Howard called every day, apologizing for his attitude and his words, but I

CATHY JO

tried not to hear any of it. I had fallen for the okey-doke too many times. This time around, if there was any leaving to be done, I was gonna be the one to do it. If that phone conversation had revealed anything to me, it was that I didn't know Howard as well as I thought. And he didn't know me.

On the day I was moving out of my parents' house, Howard showed up with a moving van full of furniture. I was stunned. My parents had tried to give me their brand-new basement furniture, but I refused to take it. I had already taken so much from them. Anyway, I was beginning to see this new phase in my life as an opportunity to turn my life around and make a fresh start. I had stopped taking the money that Howard had been giving me to help out with Shania and Jarrod and had started working a lot of overtime to make up for the difference. I was still a little short, but since I qualified for state aid (cash assistance and the Supplemental Nutrition Assistance Program), I knew I would be okay. My parents were worried about us, but I knew that their door was always open if things got too rough.

"What are you doing here?" I said to Howard as he got out of the U-Haul truck.

"I brought you something," he said, a big cheesy grin plastered across his face. He lifted the latch on the back door of the truck, and the smell of new furniture greeted me. He had bought furniture, he said, from some furniture store in North Carolina. The couch and the sofa were rich burgundy leather, and the dining set was black lacquer. Two of my favorite colors.

"You can take it back to wherever you got it from. I don't want it," I said, turning to walk back to my car, where me and my cousin Sunny had been loading boxes. Sunny shook her head, rolled her eyes at me, and mouthed the words "You trippin'" before going back into the house to get more boxes.

"I can't take it back, Tam," Howard said. "Besides, it's not for you, it's for the kids. You might not care about sitting on crates to eat your meals or watch television, but the kids shouldn't have to." He slammed down the hatch and locked it.

"Who said we would be sitting on crates? We have beds," I protested.

"Come on, Tam. Stop trying to be hard. Just take the furniture and we'll call it a loan until you can buy your own."

That sounded reasonable, I thought. To Howard I said, "Whatever," and kept moving so that we could be done and I could start unpacking boxes at my new place.

Two months after the move, I officially broke up with Howard. Even though Howard called Jarrod almost every day, Jarrod missed Howard and would ask me about him constantly. After a while he was beginning to sound like a scratched CD, and I was getting tired of telling him that Howard had to go bye-bye.

One Friday afternoon Shania was asleep in her bed and Jarrod and I were snuggled up on the couch watching *Toy Story 2*, waiting for Howard to come and take Jarrod to the car show, when the doorbell and the phone rang at the same time. "That's Howard," I told Jarrod as he ran to the door and I reached to answer the telephone. "Make sure you ask who it is before you open it."

I picked up the telephone, and the voice on the other end was Howard's, saying that he was running late but that he would be here in the next hour. I looked with alarm at Jarrod as he struggled to open the door. I jumped up, yanked his hand off the knob, and squinted through the peephole. My throat felt as though I had swallowed the Sahara desert, and my heart went on strike. Jarrod, excited that Howard was taking him to see cars, pushed my hand from the doorknob and tried again to get the door open. "Go sit down, Jarrod, okay? It's not Howard," I whispered. He looked at me with sad eyes filling with tears, and I quickly assured him that Howard had called on the phone to say that he was on his way. He must have sensed that something was wrong, because instead of sitting, Jarrod wrapped his little arms around my leg and stood protectively at my side. "I'm okay, Jarrod, really. Can you be a big boy and sit over there on the couch for Mommy?" He did as I asked, his eyes never leaving the door. Strange behavior; I had never seen him act this way before.

I opened the door and there stood Reggie Clark, all six-foot-three-inches of him, looking as beautiful as he had the day he walked out of my life. Seeing him brought back a flood of memories, and I felt like I was in high school all over again.

"Hey sexy," Reggie said, as if I had just seen him yesterday. "Can I come in, or are we gonna have this reunion in the hallway?"

Reggie always was easy with conversation. That's what I'd missed most about him when he left. I opened the door and invited him inside. "How'd you get my address?" I said, closing the door behind him.

"I got my ways." He eyed me up and down. "I see you still got that slammin' body!"

I didn't say anything. I was too busy holding my breath, waiting for him to notice Jarrod. As if on cue, Jarrod snaked his way over to me and planted himself right at my side. Reggie looked down, and I could see his whole demeanor change. He became serious, and his mouth fell open. Jarrod stared up at him, no clue who this man with the big hands was. Jarrod's hands were like a vice around my thigh. He turned his face away from Reggie, buried it between my legs, and started to whimper. I rubbed his back and shoulders until I felt his grip loosen a little. Reggie was standing there taking it all in. I could tell his feelings were hurt by the way he was biting his lower lip. Some things never changed.

"Jarrod," I said, attempting to pry his fingers from my thigh. "Can you turn around and say hello?"

"No!" he said.

"Please? I want you to meet someone." The harder I tried, the more stubborn he got. I couldn't be mad at him because he got that stubborn streak from me. I was starting to feel sorry for Reggie. He wouldn't win any father of the year awards, but the fact that he had made an effort should have netted him something. I had listened to my dad talk so much about investment banking over the years that I was starting to sound like him.

Even though Reggie wasn't a part of my son's life, he did send him cards with money in them twice a year—Christmas and his birthday. Still, no matter how I looked at it, it was just a token. Money was never a substitute for being there.

Jarrod eventually did turn around and after I explained who Reggie was, the two of them managed to have a nice visit. While we waited for Howard, I pressed Reggie for the reason for his visit. He told me that he had just graduated from the police academy, and now that he was gonna be making decent cheddar, he wanted to be a part of Jarrod's life and maybe mine too. I didn't know what to say to that last part; it was totally unexpected. So I told him that we could work something out for him to get to know Jarrod. Even as we were making plans for Reggie to come spend time with Jarrod next weekend, in the back of my mind I kept thinking about how Howard would react when I told him. We were no longer a couple, but Howard loved Jarrod and treated him like a son. Thinking of Howard in that way had me suddenly wishing that Reggie would leave. I didn't want a confrontation when Howard showed up, and I knew that there would be. As soft-spoken and laid back as Howard is, he's protective of my children and would do anything to keep them from being hurt.

From where I sat on the couch, I could see Howard's SUV pull into the parking lot. The living room window was open, and I could hear him bumpin' Nelly on his car stereo.

The palms of my hands were wet from nerves and my tongue felt heavy. I took a deep breath and hoped for the best. When the knock came, I excused myself and opened the door. Jarrod bolted from the couch and ran to Howard. Howard picked Jarrod up and stepped cautiously into the apartment. He greeted me and eyed Reggie with suspicion. I introduced them and immediately Howard's jaw set. I remember thinking, *Oh my God!*

I was relieved when Reggie said he had to be going. As he reached out his hand for Howard to shake, I couldn't help noticing the differences between them. Each man was everything the other wasn't, except in height they were nearly the same.

"It was good to see you again, Tammy," Reggie said, giving me a bear hug and a kiss on the cheek. On the way to my cheek, his lips brushed mine and I stiffened. His lips were still as soft as butter and I still felt safe in his arms, the way I used to when were dating. "I'll see you next weekend," he said, releasing me and closing the door behind him.

Howard put Jarrod down and told him to go get his jacket. "What was that all about?" he said, turning to me. "You going out with him now?"

I told Howard what it was all about and he bugged out. As bad as I felt for Howard, the truth was Reggie was Jarrod's father. He was making an effort, and he deserved a chance to get to know his son. I didn't want to be one of those women who held a grudge against the man and punished the child for the father's mistake. But if he screwed up this time, he wouldn't get another chance.

True to his word, Reggie showed up the next week, and the week after that, and the week after that, and so on. For two months straight, he showed up right after his Saturday shift ended and came to spend time with Jarrod. His son was warming up to him ,and to my surprise so was I.

I got used to having him around again, but Shania wasn't feeling Reggie at all. A couple of times he tried to play with her, but she cried if he just looked like he was going to touch her. In spite of Shania's tears, in a weird sort of way, I was starting to feel like we were a family.

Maybe it was that feeling of familiarity that made me say yes when Reggie asked me out to dinner. We were stopped at a red light on Chagrin Road on our way to the restaurant when I happened to look over into the car next to us, and there was Howard with some woman. I didn't want it to be obvious that I was peeping, so I played it off and pretended to notice for the first time the Stein Mart store that had been there for years. The SUV's windows were semi-tinted, so it was hard for me to get a good look, but I could tell by her long legs that she was tall.

When Reggie came back into the picture, Howard didn't come around as much, but he still called Jarrod and Shania every day. It had been almost two months since I had seen him, and my heart sort of leaped at the sight of him. What was that all about?

Later that night, getting ready for bed, my mind drifted back to the woman in the SUV. Was she a relative, a friend, a stranger, a lover, what? Had Howard really moved on? How could he? My kids still loved him like a father. Shania still called him Da-da. He still visited my parents like we were still dating. I had to know who that woman was, and I knew just the person to ask.

My cousin Sunny is like a bloodhound—give her just a whiff of a story and she can track down the details. I don't know how she did it, but she got the 4-1-1. She even found out what the woman's GPA was in college.

Anyway, the mystery woman's name was Sabrina Styles, and she worked at the same hospital as Howard. She was twenty-four, and they had been going out for almost a month. If it was any of the other knuckleheads I had dated, I would say that she was just a placeholder until the next female came along. But Howard wasn't a player; he took relationships seriously. If he had being going out with her for a month, then he was definitely getting serious about her. That revelation had me second-guessing my decision to break up with Howard.

After Sunny had laid that information on me, I had tossed and turned all night, trying to figure out what I was doing with my life. I was digging Reggie coming around to spend time with Jarrod, and I could even see us hookin' up again, maybe. But one thing about that was bothering me: I didn't want to get into anything with Reggie until I knew for sure that Howard and I were really done.

The next day I dropped the kids at Sunny's house and went up to Howard's job to surprise him for lunch. I was looking real fly that day. I had on my little red mini swing skirt with my white knotted-tie belly shirt showing off my pierced navel. I can do that 'cause I keep my body tight. Earlier that day I had gotten a manicure and a pedicure. My fingernails and toenails were polished fire engine red to match my skirt, and I had my hair in soft curls framing my face.

I sat in my car, listening to a Jaheim CD, waiting for Howard to go to lunch. He always took lunch between 12:15 and 12:30, and he always went out to eat because he hates cafeteria food and doesn't like packing a lunch. I waited for about an hour. The heat rising from the ground coupled with the sweet melody of Jaheim's crooning caused me to doze for a minute. Just in time, I looked up, and there he was within 50 yards of my car, with "Miss Thang" hanging all on him, like she owned him or something. I threw open the door of my Corolla and walked up to him, looking and smelling all good. By the way Howard's eyes slid nervously from the top of my head to the red-and-white rhinestone-embellished flip-flops I wore, I couldn't tell if he was pleased with what he saw or shocked that I was there. Doesn't matter. Anyway, "Miss Thang" gave me a real nasty look, like I had interrupted something. I guess Howard had told her about me. I pulled him to the side and told him that we needed to talk. At first he acted like he didn't want to. That was cool; I wasn't gonna sweat him or anything like that. We were broken up, and he didn't owe me an explanation.

"What's up, Tam?" Howard said, sounding worried. "The kids okay?"

"Yeah, they good." I was perturbed. It always had to be about my kids. "What about asking me if I'm okay? You care more about my kids than you do about me." Most people might've seen that as a plus, but right then it was all about me.

"You made it clear that I'm not welcome in your life. It's been almost four months; I have a life to live and so do you," he said, then added, "What, Mr. Universe ain't taking care of business?"

"Reggie is Jarrod's father, that's all." I searched his face for any hint that he still felt something for me. Last night I had rehearsed over and over what I would say, but standing there in front of him, I couldn't bring myself to say any of the words; it felt too much like I would be begging.

"Yeah. Whatever," Howard said. He stared at me. "Look, is there something in particular you wanted? Because I've got plans." He pulled his eyes from me and looked over at his date, who was clearly getting impatient. She looked in our direction, and when she caught Howard's eye, she tapped her watch and pursed her lips.

"Nope," I said, feeling deflated. "I got what I came for."

***

Feeling rejected by Howard, I went out with Reggie a few times, but my heart wasn't really in it, so I told him that we should just keep it about Jarrod. He agreed and said he wasn't really looking for anything too heavy.

I had just come home from working a thirteen-hour shift at the auto parts store, and the last thing I wanted was company. Howard had called me earlier in the day and asked if he could come by to see the kids. It had been a while since he had seen them, so I told him it was okay. I had just gotten out of the shower when the doorbell rang. I quickly dried off, threw on my sweats, and went to let Howard in. When I opened the door, all I saw was this huge bouquet of roses and a big red-and-white stuffed teddy bear.

Later that night, after Jarrod and Shania were in bed, Howard and I talked and we eventually made up.

***

I'm anxious for this workday to be over. When I walk out those doors tonight, the next time I walk through them it'll be as a customer and not a cashier.

Today I got a phone call from the Orange City School District telling me that I got the job. Seven months ago I applied for a job as a school bus driver, and they weren't hiring at the time, but because I knew someone who knew someone, I was allowed to take the driving test anyway. I passed the test and had a physical and the FBI background check; then they put my application on hold until something came open. Last week I got the call to come in for an interview.

When I was pregnant with Shania, I took a commercial driver's license course just for the heck of it. Getting my CDL was no joke. On the days I wasn't working, I was sitting in class three times a week, four hours a day, for twelve weeks. Some of my classmates thought it was stupid of me to be trying to get a CDL while I was pregnant. They didn't know me well enough to say that. One thing I can't stand is for somebody to tell me what I shouldn't or can't do. That drives me to want to do it, just to prove them wrong. To tell the truth, sometimes I thought I was a little crazy too. I wasn't gonna let them know that, though.

I remember the instructor's face when I climbed into that big eighteen-wheeler, belly as big as two basketballs. He was so red in the face; it looked like he'd swallowed a turnip. Shoot, my stomach was so big, I had to put the seat all the way back, and then my feet barely touched the pedals. I'm not gonna lie, it was as hard as I don't know what. But I passed on the first try. Looks like it's finally going to pay off.

***

When Howard and I got back together, I quit my job at the auto parts store when I found out I was pregnant. I was determined not to be more of a burden than I already felt I was, so I looked for less strenuous work. When I had first started job-hunting, nobody would hire me. I went everywhere. Maybe it was because I was six months pregnant. I had pretty much decided that since I wasn't going to be working, I'd go back to school. I was on the verge of registering for winter semester when Mr. Jones from QualMart called and asked me if I was still interested in the job. I took the job, but a day before my ninety days were up, I went into labor. I thought for sure that I wouldn't be able to take maternity leave and come back, but Mr. Jones hooked it up for me.

We've butted heads a lot during the time I've been here, and it's mainly because I'm not down with that jungle fever thing he has for all the black female employees. When I first started working here, he used to be all up in my grill, talking about what all he could do for me. When I complained to his boss about him, Mr. Jones started giving me grief about my schedule. I put up with all that nonsense because I had bills to pay and I needed the money. Now that I've accomplished my goal, what I really want to do is go in Mr. Jones's office and tell him to kiss where the sun don't shine. That's what I would like do, but I won't. Even though he's a weasel, I feel indebted to him for taking a chance on me when nobody else would. Besides, my granddad always tells me not to burn bridges because you never know when you'll have to cross them again.

During the time I was on maternity leave, Howard kept telling me that I didn't have to work; he would take care of me. I couldn't let him do that. I pay my own way. Besides, even though he loves my kids like they're his, it wouldn't be fair to put that on him. He's a good provider and a good father to my kids, and I didn't want him to start seeing us as burdens. Jarrod and Shania are crazy about Howard. I thought that once Howard Jr. was born, he would start treating the kids differently, but he doesn't. When he buys Howard Jr. toys or clothes or anything else, he makes sure he has something for Jarrod and Shania too.

My parents are so impressed with Howard. I tease my mom that she only likes him because he's an RN like her. She says that's only partly true, but she also likes him because he keeps me centered. I have to say I agree with her. My parents are real cool people. Although they've been married for twenty-seven years, you couldn't tell it by watching them: they act like newlyweds. If I ever do get married, that's the kind of relationship I want with my husband. My dad likes Howard because, as he says, "That boy knows how to take care of business." In more ways than one, if my daddy only knew.

When I get home tonight, I think I'll fix Howard a nice meal so that we can celebrate my good news and to show him that I love him. We've been through a testing phase and came out better for it.

A few months after we got back together, Howard wanted to move in together, but we eventually decided against it. It just wouldn't feel right. He didn't like the neighborhood I was living in, and I couldn't afford a better place. So he decided that he would help me with living expenses. Thankfully, I was able to get off public assistance.

Reggie is even giving me money for Jarrod. It's not a lot of money (he has three other children to take care of), but it is steady. Howard would rather we did everything through the court system, but this way is okay with me. A few times Reggie tried to get close to me. I won't lie; it was tempting, but right now, my mind is on Howard.

I think God sending me Howard was his way of telling me that there still are good men in the world. I've learned that looks can fade and the body can break down, but it's what you are in the inside that's most important. My man, Howard, is a beautiful, loving man. I really want this relationship to work out. Considering that none of my other kids' daddies stayed longer than six months, Howard is a saint.

When my shift ends I'm going to pick up all the ingredients for Howard's favorite meal: T-bone steak, potatoes, onions, salad fixings, a nice domestic wine (read: cheap), and for dessert, strawberry shortcake. We'll drop the kids at my cousin's house, or my parents' if Sunny can't babysit. While the food is cooking, I'll burn those jasmine-scented candles that he likes so much. I'll take a quick shower, then put on my black, form-fitting strapless mini dress that flares slightly at the hem. The dress was a gift to myself for passing the CDL test. I'm getting excited just thinking about it!

For all he does for me, I don't mind pampering my man. Not just moneywise either. Howard has always been supportive of me in whatever I wanted to do. He's not like some men who try to hold their women back, thinking their manhood is being threatened. When I told Howard I wanted to go back to school, he told me that he would pay for it. I appreciated the gesture, but when I do go back, I'll be paying my own way. That has to be my victory and mine alone.

As I'm sitting in one of the smaller break rooms thinking about my plans for the night, Maurice, the store clown, sneaks up behind me and taps me on my right shoulder, although he's standing at my left. I fall for that trick every time.

"What us gon' do you when you leave, Miss Tamyla? The plantation won't be the same without you." He shuffles over to a chair and flops down in it.

I burst out laughing. "Plantation" is the nickname I gave the store because that's the way the owners run the place. Black, white, yellow, brown, it doesn't matter; we're all treated like slaves. "You crazy, Mo!" I say, wiping tears of laughter from my face. "I'm gonna miss you," I say, sad-faced.

"I'll miss you too," he says, throwing an arm around my shoulder. He looks around the break room conspiratorially and whispers under his breath, "Massa give you yo' freedom papers yet?"

I fall on the floor laughing.

Maurice shuffles out of the break room, looking over his shoulders, and I go to clean out my locker.

Janice comes and tells me that Mr. Jones wants to see me, something about an exit interview. *An exit interview?* I stop cleaning out my locker and go to see what's up. I sit there listening to my soon-to-be former boss drone on about what a pleasure it was having a team member with my dedication work for him. He tries to talk me into staying, just on weekends, but I had to pass, of course. I am mother, after all, and I have a life. I'm not even tryin' to work that hard. I leave his office feeling free.

I head back to the break room, where the lockers are, to put my "freedom papers"—I mean, a copy of my exit interview—in my locker so that I can go say good-bye to a few people. Janice, Sue, and a few other co-workers jump out of nowhere yelling, "Surprise!" and almost scare me to death. After I pick my heart up off the floor, I'm sorta touched. They almost make me cry. I can't believe that in the short time it took for my exit interview, they decorated a few tables in the break room, complete with party favors and my favorite snack foods: pretzels, mini corn dogs, root beer, cheese popcorn, and raspberry Cassata cake. I'm sure the cake was Janice's idea; she's one the most thoughtful people I know. I'll really miss Janice. Her sweet thoughtfulness reminds me a lot of my mom.

I'll even miss Sue. My first week at QualMart, Sue and I got off on the wrong foot, but we're fine now. She thought that I would be a pushover because I was young and pregnant. But she quickly found out that she was wrong. She had brought a leftover half of a Subway sandwich from home one day, and somebody stole it out of the refrigerator. When she saw me eating half of a Subway sandwich that Howard had split with me when he met me on my morning break, she went sideways. She got all up in my face, calling me this and that, saying I was ghetto and that I was a thief. I got right back in her face and gave as good as I got, and even better. It was ugly. Come to find out, Benita, the head cashier, had thrown Sue's sandwich in the garbage to make up for Sue filing a complaint against her earlier that day because Benita kept scheduling Sue to work till closing every night of the week, even though the rules say that no one is supposed to close more than three nights in a row. Two weeks later, Sue apologized, and we've been cool ever since.

I'm not big on hugging men, but when Chuck, a mildly mentally disabled stock boy, hugs me good-bye, I don't mind. Touchy-feely James from the deli department tries the same thing, but I squash that and shake his hand instead. Even though I'm looking forward to starting my new job and meeting new people, I will miss a lot of the people at QualMart. You know how it is when you work around a lot of people: some you like and some you can do without.

As the party winds down, I hug Janice, Sue, and Maurice and promise to keep in touch, then thank everyone for their thoughtfulness and go to finish emptying my locker. I need to hurry up. My shift ends in ten minutes, and Howard and the kids will be here soon. Usually I drive myself to work, but since this was my last day, Howard thought I would be "too emotional" to drive. Besides, today is his day off, and he volunteered to watch the kids. I thought that was so sweet of him. Just then I remember that we're supposed to be going to the movies, Howard and me. My mom has agreed to come over and watch the kids for us. I'll have to put a hold on that special dinner until tomorrow night.

"Mommy, mommy!" Jarrod and Shania yell out the window, as I approach the car. I see Howard reach in the back to open the car door for Jarrod to get out but my son is having none of it. "I'll do it," he says, pushing unsuccessfully on the door. He's at that age where he needs to assert his independence. Shania is fussing in her car seat because she can't get loose. I open the car door, and Jarrod bursts out, holding his hands out for me to pick him up. So much for independence.

"Did you miss Mommy today?" I ask, planting big sloppy kisses on his cheek. I give Shania and Howard Jr. the same sloppy kisses and hugs. Shania has my neck in a vice grip, competing for my attention, and Howard Jr. grins and slobbers. Jarrod talks incessantly about what he and Howard did today as I put him safely back into the car and fasten his seat belt.

"Hi, sweetheart," I say to Howard, smooching him before getting into the car. If I hadn't stopped him, Howard would still be opening doors and pulling out chairs for me. Not that I don't like that; I just don't think it needs to be something he does *every* time. "What's this?" I ask, eyeing the blue duffle bag on the floor.

"That's a change of clothes," Howard admits. "Since your parents' house is on the way to the movies, I thought that we could take the kids there and you could shower and change over there, rather than backtracking and wasting gas going home." He gives me a sneaky look.

I'm not crazy about the idea: I'm tired and wanted to relax a little, since I wouldn't be cooking. But I can see that he's put a lot of thought into it, so I high-five him and go along with it.

When we get to my parents' house, Jarrod and Shania run wild, like they don't have any home training. Me and Mom try to quiet them while Daddy plays with Howard Jr. and Howard plays with the TV remote.

"Listen up, everybody," Howard says; he's now standing in the middle of the living room with his hands stuffed in his pockets. He tells Jarrod and Shania to stop running around and come into the living room and sit down. They obey him without so much as a whimper. "Mr. Bradford," Howard says, looking Daddy dead in the eye. "You know how much I respect and admire you. You're like a second father to me."

He's putting up a front to be brave, but I can tell that he's a little nervous. *About what, though?* I wonder. *Oh no! Is this what I think it is? Oh my God, no! He must've planned this. I hope this doesn't mean that we're not going to the movies; I was really looking forward to seeing the new Will Smith flick. What am I thinking?* I'm so nervous, I can hardly breathe.

Howard is still talking. "When I met your daughter four years ago, I had no way of knowing that I was getting more than a gorgeous, caring, self-sacrificing woman; I was getting a family. That's what you and your wife have become to me." Howard doesn't crack a smile. I can't remember the last time I saw my man so serious.

I look over at my mother, and she's beaming from head to toe. My daddy is sitting there with his chest puffed out, holding the baby.

"If it's okay with you, sir," Howard continues, "I'd like to ask your permission to have your daughter's hand in marriage." Howard's hands have found their way out of his pockets, and now they're balled up like fists at his sides, the way they always are when he's *really* nervous.

At this point my mouth is wide open, and I'm totally in shock.

My daddy, always the joker, says, "Take her, boy! We've got no use for her anymore."

"Sydney!" my mother scolds.

"You know I'm just joking, Vera." My daddy clears his throat and gets serious. "Mr. Coleman it would be both an honor and a pleasure to give you my daughter's hand in marriage." Then he grins. "Of course, I don't know how she feels about that." We all laugh; Jarrod and Shania laugh the loudest. *Kids.*

Howard walks over to where I'm sitting and gets down on one knee. I look at him in astonishment; I just can't believe this is happening. Tears are streaming down my face. He reaches in the pocket of his jeans, pulls out a velvet box, and opens it. My eyes open so wide that I don't think I'll ever be able to close them again. I gasp when I see the big, white rock staring at me. Wow! I don't know anything about diamonds and how much they weigh, but this is *the* biggest diamond I have ever seen. If my engagement ring looks like this, I wonder what the wedding ring will look like!

"Baby," Howard begins, "even though we've had our ups and downs, we've always come out on top, and our relationship is rock solid. Before I met you, I always felt like a part of me was missing. Now I know that that part was you. I love Jarrod and Shania like they are my own, and I love you for sharing them with me. I can't see myself going through life without you all. You are my woman, my friend, my life. Tamyla Gwen Bradford, will you be my wife?"

Howard's eyes are fixated on me as he nervously awaits my answer. I look over at Jarrod and Shania, and they're both sitting quietly next to my parents. My son Howard Jr. is nestled in my daddy's arms. What more could I ask for? This man not only loves me and my kids, he loves my parents too. That makes me love him even stronger.

I try the name out on my tongue: "Tamyla Gwen Coleman," I whisper. I love the sound of that! My tear-streaked face breaks out into a cheesy grin, and that's all the confirmation Howard needs.

THREE CARDS SHORT OF A DECK

I DON'T KNOW HOW LONG I'VE BEEN HERE. TIME HAS NO relevance anymore.

The room we're in is suffocatingly small; the windows do not open. Floral, lined drapes hang limply at the barred windows. White brick walls cage us in—a fortress. The door, which can only be opened from the outside, is heavy, like steel. It has a pane of glass at least three inches thick. Crisscrossing through it is what looks like wire, probably to ensure that we don't escape this hell. The floor is concrete, painted gray. In the middle of the room is a long table that takes up half the space in the room. The table reminds me of the one in the boardroom of the corporation where I used to work as Chief Financial Officer.

Every year around this time, the news stations do a follow-up piece on my story, and every year they've dogged me for an interview. My usual response was to reject their promise of unbiased coverage. Today, however, I've broken my self-imposed silence and agreed to allow the well-known reporter Miranda Bosch to interview me. After weeks of negotiating, we were finally able to agree on acceptable terms for the interview; she is only to ask questions through my team of doctors, and she's not to speak to me unless I give her permission.

As we—Dr. Ashton, Dr. Oliver, Dr. Henderson, the reporter, and me—take our seats, I'm hoping that she doesn't misquote me. The cameraman, who is sort of cute for a white man, hoists his camera on his shoulder and instructs us where to sit. The reporter opens a manila folder and pushes two newspaper clippings at me; I want to push her. The headlines read:

"MAN'S BRUTALLY SLAIN BODY DISCOVERED BY NEIGHBOR!"

"WIFE KILLS HUSBAND, SITS DOWN TO A CUP OF JAVA!"

My throat constricts, and for a split second I feel panicky. I thought I had seen all the lies. I pull a cigarette from the open package lying on the table. We're not allowed to have matches or lighters, so I wait for one of the doctors to give me a light. I inhale the sweet nectar of menthol, now feeling reflective and in control.

"My friends call me Arlie," I say to the reporter. "My mother named me Arlise; I prefer the name Janice. But who's complaining?" I say in my best Groucho Marx imitation. "Of course, you already know my name. Who's left on the planet who doesn't know my name? Or face, for that matter?" I look, with somber eyes, at the cameraman and see him chuckle. Quickly, he composes himself.

"You news reporters made all sorts of assumptions about my mental state," I say, a menacing expression on my face. I want the reporter to know that I'm not to be toyed with. "Are you one of them?" I ask her. She shakes her head no, vigorously. Holding the cigarette between my middle finger and index finger, I twirl it slowly, round and round, with my thumb, careful not to burn myself. I take a puff. "One reporter said that I 'must have been suffering from some sort of repressed memory disorder.' As if I care what he thinks." I flick my ashes into the ashtray; some miss and land on the reporter's skirt. She smiles coldly and politely brushes them away. "Ever since that self-important reporter made that statement," I continue, "I've heard that term, *repressed memory disorder*, quite often.

"As usual," I continue, "they've got it all wrong." A barely perceptible smirk raises a corner of the reporter's mouth, and I roll my eyes. "What I suffer from is called Post Traumatic Stress Disorder." The reporter's eyes twinkle, and it looks to me as though she's salivating, waiting for the next morsel. "You do know what that is, PTSD, don't you?" I ask. She looks in the direction of my team of doctors (I don't know why she does that) and shakes her head yes. "In my case," I explain, "Dr. Ashton says a trauma suffered in my 'formative years'—his words, not mine—spent with my aunt Annabelle is the cause of my *alleged*—my word, not his—PTSD."

As I'm repeating Dr. Ashton's assessment of me and my situation, I'm imitating his deep, frog-like voice, like Froggy from the Little Rascals, gravelly and scratched. I must do a good job, because they all laugh, even Dr. Ashton. I also mention that I'm being assessed for bipolar disorder and some other disorders that we don't need to get into. That admission earns me a bug-eyed stare of incredulity from the blonde-haired wannabe super sleuth.

"His theory sounds good, has all the right buzzwords, but I'm not buying any of it. Head doctors—you know, shrinks—always try to blame people's behaviors on one catastrophic event or another. No offense, Doctors," I say, raising my hand in mock apology. "But sometimes people just do things, and it has nothing to do with their childhood. Don't take that statement as an admission of guilt," I warn. Dr. Henderson scribbles something in his notepad.

Miranda Bosch tries to interject a question. Putting a finger to my lips, I hush her and remind her that the only reason I agreed to this interview is because lies are being told, and spreading like gangrene, about me and my family, and I want to clear my people's names.

"Here's how it's going to go," I say, the cigarette dangling precariously from the tip of my lower lip. "Remember, you will speak only on my say-so, and you will ask only questions permitted by my team. I'm going to set the record straight once and for all about my upbringing and my family. Make sure you're paying attention, because once I say something, I will *not* repeat it." I see anger flash in her eyes and she shifts in her seat, upset that I'm in control of this interview. "After I'm finished talking," I continue, "you'll see that everything you thought you knew about me and my family are all lies. So pay attention, Mi-ran-*da*." Although I direct my comments to the reporter, I'm hoping that my doctors will take note as well, because I'm well past ready to be done with "treatment" so I can go home.

"Sure," I begin, saying this with the air of a dignitary, "my aunt was serious when it came to raising children, but she was no worse than any other parent. My brother and sister and I never wanted for anything. We were well taken care of." I pause, allowing everyone time to digest this information. "We went to live with my aunt when I was three and Alvin was five. My father was killed in a car accident when my baby sister was just six months. Because of that accident, my mother suffered a nervous breakdown, and from what I heard, she was never quite right after that. She committed suicide some years later. So all the rumors and speculation you reporters are spreading about how I was really the love child of my father and my aunt, and that my aunt agreed to raise my mother's children because of the guilt she felt about the affair, are all lies!"

"Calm down, Arlise," Dr. Oliver says in his soothing voice, his meaty jowls looking like someone stuffed them with sausages.

"Can you tell me—?"

The reporter tries to interject a question, but I silence her with a glare. She broke the rules and didn't get permission to speak.

I'm sure they don't know this about my aunt Annabelle, so I tell them. "My auntie, who is my mother's sister, stepped in and took over so that we wouldn't become wards of the court. What she did was heroic, don't you think?" They all nod in unison. They look like those little bobble head toy dogs that you sometimes see in the back windows of some people's cars. "She was grieving herself, you know. Her husband, my uncle Frank, died in that car accident, too. He was driving drunk." I feel my shoulders droop from the weight of that revelation and quickly sit up straight, careful not to show any sign of weakness.

Thinking of my baby sister, I smile. "Miriam was a real character when she was younger She once told me that having me for a big sister made her feel special. You see, when we were younger, whenever I wanted to do something that we knew my auntie would be dead set against, Miriam was my biggest advocate. She had ulterior motives, of course. She knew that if I got to do something, then she would too when her turn came." I stop to assess the effect of my words on the group. Nothing.

"I'm proud of my sister. From the time we were children, she saved most of her money so that she could go to college, and what she hadn't saved she worked for in order to put herself through college. She was refused a loan from the bank where I worked, but she never took a dime of my husband's and my money when *he* offered to help her with tuition." I stress the word *he*, making it understood that I had nothing to do with my husband's offer of money to my baby sister. "The lie you reporters keep spreading about how the money he offered her was hush money to keep quiet about fraudulent bank practices that I was supposedly trying to cover up is vicious and unfounded. It was bribery money to get her to talk against me. But my sister is honest through and through, and she would never conspire with anyone to tell lies on me."

The reporter leans over and whispers something to my team of doctors, and they all nod their agreement.

At this point, I allow the golden-haired newshound to ask me a question.

"Although you've maintained your innocence from the beginning, a jury of seven women and five men returned a verdict of guilty at your trial. Do you feel any remorse for what happened to your husband?" she asks, her pencil at the ready to jot down my answer.

I stare blankly at her, take a slow, erotic drag on my Benson & Hedges, and blow wedding rings of smoke in the direction of the cameraman. That's the sixty-four-thousand-dollar question. Everyone wants me to admit to something I didn't do. I suppose as far as I'm concerned, my husband got what he deserved. I warned him what would happen. I don't say this because I don't want my statement misconstrued in any way.

"People tell me I have an old soul; they say I act like I'm ninety years old," I say, ignoring Goldie's ridiculous question. "I suppose that to some degree they might have a point, but what is an *old soul*?" Golden-hair looks at me, and then at Dr. Oliver, who shrugs in confusion, a stupid, befuddled expression on her face. I ignore her; she's beginning to irritate me.

"By that, do they mean I'm wise beyond my forty-two years, or that I'm not lively enough, bubbly enough?" I ask and sigh. Already I'm bored, though they've only been here twenty minutes. The reporter looks at me questioningly, as though trying to find the right answer. How would she know the answer to that question? I didn't really expect her to; it was rhetorical. *What an imbecile.* I wave my hand dismissively in her direction.

As the reporter waits for me to continue, her pencil dances the mambo in her hand, hungry for whatever scrap I'm about to throw her way.

"I remember one time when Miriam was eight," I say, as I shift in the gray metal institution chair with its puffy cushioned seat. "The teacher called home because Miriam was acting up in class, making faces at her friend Shelly while the teacher was at the blackboard. You know, kid stuff. Aunt Annabelle didn't believe in children misbehaving in class, so without a doubt, she was hot when she put the phone down. We all knew what was coming. I ran to the left, into the living room. My brother Alvin darted to the right, the dining room. Poor little Miriam hid under the kitchen table, not ten feet from where Auntie was standing. I suppose she thought that huge table would protect her. It didn't. I could see her little face. She looked like a scared rabbit, lips quivering, from where I hid behind that ugly, brown couch."

At this point I have to pause, because the image of my baby sister writhing on the floor in pain is too real. "I can hear Auntie's voice now, like she's right here with me saying, 'If I have to tell you one mo' time to git me a switch, I'm gon' slap the black off you!'" I say, mimicking my auntie's nicotine-soaked voice, raspy, raw, and throaty. "Short—that's what we called her behind her back—didn't play. She'd sooner snatch you bald than repeat herself." Dr. Ashton, Dr. Oliver, and the reporter exchange questioning glances. Dr. Henderson gets it; he's black like me.

"When I was about seven or eight, I learned that if I wanted to live to see my next birthday, I had to develop supersonic hearing, or else get down on my knees every night and pray to the Good Lord to deliver me from the wrath of Annabelle Tyler. I did both, just in case one failed." This time, I notice the reporter stifle a laugh. It seems funny now, but back then it was no joke. I used to have nightmares.

"I was sort of scared of Short. She was a big, strong woman with an imposing presence. She hit me one time, and that was all it took for me to be as good as gold the rest of my childhood." I give a hearty laugh and again light a fresh cigarette from the butt of my old one. Goldie lets out a fake cough, a hint that my smoking bothers her. My husband had the same annoying, judgmental habit. *Why don't you just come out and tell me you don't like the smoke?* I think as I blow a cloud of it in her direction.

"My auntie was really a good woman deep down, way down. She made you work extra hard to find her goodness, but when you did, it was like sunshine on a cold day." I close my eyes, trying to feel the rays of her sun. When I open my eyes, I see Dr. Henderson again jotting something down in his notebook. More conjecture, I guess. What an annoying habit. It reminds me of the journal that Aunt Annabelle was always writing in.

"Let me give you a for instance," I say slowly, methodically. The cameraman brings the camera in closer. "We were on our way back from church one Sunday afternoon. I must've been, oh, about twelve or so, and some boy yelled something profane from the window of an ugly pea-green Ford LTD at my brother Alvin. Before I knew it, I was yelling after him that it was the Lord's Day and that he ought to have more respect for my auntie. Short didn't smile much back then, but I saw her beam that day."

The reporter, on the edge of her seat by now, irritated from the smoke and anxious to ask me another question, fidgets with her notepad and chews the eraser on the end of her pencil. I debate whether I should acknowledge her and decide that I'll grant her permission to speak. Dr. Oliver motions for the reporter to wait, and they again put their heads together and whisper before the doctor approves the question.

"Why did you children nickname your auntie 'Short'?" Her little girl voice is grating and distracting.

Her pencil hovers anxiously above her pad, and just as I begin to speak, the tape recorder cuts off. "Will you wait just a second while I flip the tape over?" she wants to know.

I say no and proceed to explain the nickname. Just in time, she manages to flip the tape. *Good for her*, I think. Maybe next time she'll use a digital recorder.

"It's simple. My aunt was the shortest of all her brothers and sisters. My uncle Tambo was six-foot-six; Aunt Earlin, six-four; Uncle Hersey, six-three; and my mother, Lola, six-two. Aunt Annabelle was only five-eleven." The reporter and cameraman exchange amused glances. I wonder if there's something going on between them.

Just as I am about to continue, the reporter speaks out of turn and cuts me off. "Are you sure your aunt's nickname wasn't Short because she was known around the neighborhood for having a short temper? Isn't it true that she beat you and your siblings at the least bit of provocation?"

"Ms. Bosch!" Dr. Ashton scolds. "If you do not honor the terms of our agreement, we will have to stop the interview."

Goldie apologizes, but I'm unfazed. I knew that question would come, and I was prepared for it. The weekly rag magazines had been printing that lie for years. I gave her my customary response: I ignored the question.

"I remember this one time, Miriam and I were on the side of the house, by the driveway, playing with the milk chute, when Aunt Annabelle and my cousin Maxine came strolling up the walk. I almost messed my pants, I was so scared. I glimpsed Maxine's face and caught the pity in her eyes; she knew we were about to get the beating of our lives." I chuckle. "Auntie hated for us to play with the milk chute, even more than she hated for children to be outside unsupervised. Uncle Hersey was supposed to be watching us, but he'd fallen asleep on the couch and was snoring to beat the band. I know Aunt Annabelle had to have seen us playing with the milk chute, but instead of a whipping, all she gave us was the evil eye—that look that can scare the bejesus out of a kid, making them want to grind themselves into the ground. Then she told us to 'Git on in the house!'

"I looked over at my baby sister, who had tears racing to the corners of her mouth, and grinned. I guess she couldn't turn the tear tap off soon enough, because tears were flowing like a busted water pipe." I cross, then uncross my legs, teasing the cameraman. I can tell he's interested by the way his Adam's apple keeps bobbing up and down. I can't see his eyes, but I know they're smiling.

After getting permission from the team, the reporter asks me if *I* had learned to turn off the "tear tap" at an early age. I ignore her.

"Another time," I continue, "Alvin and I wanted to go to the corner store so we could buy some penny candy—Mary Janes and

Lemonheads. You're probably too young to remember when Mary Janes were three for a penny and Lemonheads were a nickel a box," I say to the cameraman. His neck turns beet red; I assume he's blushing. "If we had enough money left over, we were going to buy a bag of Cheez Doodles and split it. We asked Uncle Hersey to walk us to the store and he said no. Flat out, just like that, no! By the way, Uncle Hersey came to live with Aunt Annabelle when her husband died. Make sure you tell your newspaper to retract the lie they've been printing about my aunt and uncle. He was her *brother, not her lover!*" I bang my hand on the table, making Golden-hair jump. I guess she didn't see that coming.

"See, Uncle Hersey didn't believe in letting children waste their chore money on junk food," I continue. "He thought that we ought to be saving for college or something useful like that. We waited just as good until we could hear him snatching his breaths and tiptoed out the back door. I thought we were caught for sure when that old, rickety, wooden screen door slammed shut. We kicked our Converse sneakers into high gear and took off running, fast! If Uncle Hersey did wake up to investigate the racket, all he saw was a cloud of dust.

"Forgive me for laughing," I say, dabbing at the wetness in the corners of my eyes with my index finger. "Every time I think of my butterball of a brother huffing and puffing, trying to keep up with me, I can't help myself. We ran there *and* back. That we managed to sneak back in unnoticed is a miracle, what with all the loud, heavy breathing coming from Alvin. It's a good thing Short was at the hairdresser's." I can hardly get the words out, I'm cracking up laughing so much. I swipe the tears of laughter from my eyes with the back of my hand and look over at the cameraman. He can hardly keep the camera still. He's shaking with laughter. The reporter is sitting in her chair stone-faced, probably upset that I wouldn't acknowledge her question. Her refusal to laugh with us must be her way of punishing me.

I ignore her wearisome moon-face and continue the interview. "Speaking of the hairdresser's," I say, "my auntie sure could wear a hairdo, until it turned into a hair-don't." More laughter from the cameraman. I think to myself, *When I get out of here, I'm going to look him up.* Maybe I can get him to slip me his number before he leaves. Still nothing from the reporter. Witch! I hate her smugness. Those pretty looks are only going to take her so far, she'll see.

"Do you feel any remorse for what you did to your husband?" she asks. This time the question is more forceful and accusatory. She spoke out of turn, again. And like before, Dr. Oliver reprimands her but Dr. Henderson cuts in, reminding Dr. Oliver that the reporter's question is a reiteration of an earlier question. Even still, I ignore her.

"On Christmas, Easter, and birthdays, we got whatever we wanted," I say, determined to make Blondie see that we were a normal family. "One year I got a life-size doll, Alvin got a new Huffy bike, and Miriam got an Easy-Bake Oven *and* a miniature Coca-Cola machine. Like I said, whatever we asked for, we got."

The reporter goes to write in her notepad and the lead in her pencil breaks. She lays the pencil on the table and pulls a pen from her purse. She clicks it open and I start. I stare at the blood red pen as she scrawls words onto the pad. As I'm watching the motion of the pen, I hear the reporter ask a question. Apparently, she's been given permission, because no one protests.

"Did your aunt Annabelle ever tell you that she loved you?"

The question catches me by surprise, and I have to think about it. I sit in silence for what feels like an eternity, pondering the question until my head hurts. Just as I'm about to speak, I hear the rapid, impatient clicking of the reporter's ink pen, and I'm transported back to my childhood when Aunt Annabelle would keep a list of our misdeeds and then punish us while we slept. That incessant clicking of the pen before she'd write down our transgressions kept me on edge for the rest of my childhood and well into my adult life. No matter how good we tried to be, Miriam and I bore the brunt of her so-called love. Once, when we came home from school five minutes late, the wire hanger that left little triangle-shaped abrasions on our torsos as she beat us into semi-consciousness was her way of showing us how much she loved us and worried about us when we broke the rules.

As I'm trying to gain control of myself, my mind flashes to the time Aunt Annabelle tied Alvin to a kitchen chair with rope and beat him across his thighs with a nine-inch skillet until he passed out from shock. To get her point across and to teach us the value of obedience, Auntie used to make us watch each other's punishment. The voyeuristic abuse went on for years: the cigarette burns, the whippings with the flat side of a butcher's knife, the glass bottle whippings on our upper arms. The neighbors always helped us children but never told the authorities. Times were different then.

Toward the end of my marriage, my husband, who knew that I didn't allow pens with levers in our home, also broke the rules. *Click, click, click.* He wouldn't stop pressing the lever. I kept screaming for him to stop and he wouldn't. Now, like then, everything is happening so quickly. Back and forth, first slowly, then a little faster, I rock. The camera is like a cannon pointed at my head. I see the blue gases concealed behind the lens, and it's about to ignite. The thought of the camera igniting and the angle at which it's projected reminds me of the belt buckle that caught me in the eye when Aunt Annabelle was whipping me because I hadn't done a thorough enough job of drying the dishes.

All voices are muffled now, tunneled. Dr. Ashton's hand coils around my forearm like a snake, and I feel myself hurl him into something. A door? A wall? I hear a noise, a thud, as his body makes contact with whatever. I'm trying to gain control, but I can't. My mind is betraying me.

Bears rush at me from every direction. Panda bears. Grizzly bears. Koala bears. They want to hug me. *How strange*, I think. I haven't been hugged in a long time. I welcome it. I feel a sudden prick on my upper arm, and slowly silence and sleep engulf me.

When I awake, the clicking sound is gone, but the reporter's words, probing and intrusive, still swim in my head: "Do you feel any remorse for what you did to your husband?" "Did your aunt Annabelle ever tell you that she loved you?" Like a wash cycle, they pummel my consciousness and reverberate incessantly. I cover my ears in an attempt to shut out the annoying words. It doesn't help. They're trapped there, embedded forever.

I clumsily stumble to the locked door of my prison room and kick feebly with the ball of my foot—the jacket has amputated my hands. I doubt that anyone will hear me. I slide to the floor, staring fixedly at the crumpled sheets on my torturously uncomfortable bed.

Feeling groggy and disconnected, I let my mind take in my surroundings: twin bed; rough charcoal-colored wool blanket; white linens; black-and-gray speckled tiles; yellow walls; wardrobe. The room is dismal and ugly, so unlike my cheery, welcoming room at home.

I sit quietly on the cold, concrete floor for hours, dissecting the interview with the blonde reporter in my head, satisfied that now that I have set the record straight about my family, I should be going home in a little while. Then I remember: I forgot to get the cameraman's phone number.

REFLECTIONS—IN MEMORIAM

IN THE QUIET SOLITUDE OF MY OFFICE, BEHIND DOORS THAT seem impenetrable, I like to reflect on my own life and the rich tapestry of tragedy that made me choose the profession I did. As we navigate the steep hills and rough terrain of our lives, both as children and as adults, I believe we eventually come up with a plan that helps us cope with the many obstacles that life has a way of putting in front of us.

My paternal grandmother, may God rest her soul, had her share plus some of steep hills and rough terrain. By the time she was eight years old, she was responsible for her three younger siblings and making sure her mother didn't double book johns. One thing I admired about my grandmother was that she wasn't shy when it came to talking about her past. Grandma Beasley would tell me all the time that if I could live my life through her eyes, then maybe I wouldn't make the mistakes she made and I would have a shot at having a good, decent life. I took those words to heart, and now I help others to navigate the rough terrains of their lives.

Thinking of my grandmother brings a pang of longing to my heart and makes me miss her all the more. Grandma Beasley used to say that when I was younger I was a holy terror. This from a woman who ran numbers, used to be a hit woman for an organized crime gang, and shot and killed a man just for speaking to her, which, incidentally, led to her spending the rest of her life behind the walls of the Ohio Reformatory for Women in

Marysville, Ohio. To be honest, I think she confused me with my older brother, Joshua.

I was a good child who never caused anybody any trouble. Joshua, on the other hand, was a holy terror if ever there was one. Compared to him, Dennis the Menace was a saint. That boy got into more than a little bit of trouble. If there were upturned trash cans, overflowing toilets, piles of dead and mutilated insects, little girls sitting in corners crying for their mommies, or general chaos and pandemonium spread throughout the neighborhood, you could bet that Joshua was somewhere lurking in the shadows, thumb stuck in his mouth, surveying the scene. The boy was just plain ol' B-A-D. Bad.

I'll never forget the time my brother and his friends, Sam and Benjamin, broke into Mr. Hezekiah's candy store and looted the place. All because Mr. Hezekiah wouldn't let him buy a twenty-five-cent can of pop for a nickel. It wasn't Mr. Hezekiah's fault that Joshua couldn't tell a quarter from a nickel.

Then there was the time Joshua and Benjamin were dropping bricks off the freeway overpass by I-90 east at the East 72nd Street exit in Cleveland. The brick that hit the brown pickup truck that a woman and two small children were riding in caused the truck to flip over several times before rolling down the embankment. Thank God nobody died, but the mother was paralyzed from the neck down, and one of the children, a girl, I believe, suffered permanent brain damage. The police never did catch the person responsible for the accident. But I knew because Joshua had confided in me and swore me to secrecy.

I hate to say this, but as bad as my brother was, he was no match for our cousin Travis. Travis was mean with his bad. He would do stuff like hit you with rocks, throw dirt in your face, or pull a knife on you and laugh at you and criticize you for crying or being fearful while he was tormenting you. Something was seriously wrong with that boy. I remember the time the whole family was going to Tennessee for a family reunion, and we pulled over at a rest stop. Everybody got out of the car to use the bathroom, get something to eat, stretch our legs, whatever, but Travis stayed behind. He was mad about something. I can't remember what; it was so long ago. Anyway, when we got back, Travis was still sitting in the car, same spot, but he had a little smirk on his face.

When Daddy tried to start the engine, the car wouldn't start. At first he thought we had run out of gas, but that wasn't it because we had just filled up a few miles back. Daddy stood there cussing and fussing at that car, calling it all kinds of names, but it still wouldn't start. Finally, he broke down and called for a tow truck. When the tow truck man came, he tried to get the car started but couldn't. Then he noticed a white and brown substance near the gas tank and went to inspect it.

"Uh, this here's your problem, sir," the tow truck driver said to Daddy as he bent over and gathered some of the brown and white substance between his fingers. He put his fingers to his tongue and tasted it. "Somebody done gone and put sugar and dirt in ya tank."

Daddy was mad then. Hoppin' mad! He got to stuttering and spitting, ranting and raving, and Travis got the butt whipping of his life. Travis had picked the lock on the trunk, taken the funnel out that Daddy used for oil changes, opened the extra bag of sugar Mama brought along for Daddy's Kool-Aid, and mixed it with dirt then poured it in the tank. We didn't make it to the family reunion that year, and Travis never did say why he did what he did.

Years later, Travis did tell me about a woman he had a crush on, whom he'd met at a bus stop. He spotted her one day while he was shopping at the supermarket that's part of the apartment complex where he lived in downtown Cleveland. She wouldn't give him the time of day, he said. When he was sure she wasn't paying attention, he followed her up to her apartment, just to see which apartment was hers. He said he tried on numerous occasions to get her interested in him, but nothing worked. He constantly bought her flowers and left them at her door, and she got a temporary restraining order against him.

Then one Valentine's Day he bought her a stuffed teddy bear and a box of chocolates and had the gifts sent to her job, which he'd followed her to several times. He just knew that would impress her. It didn't. She had him arrested for stalking. After several months of rejections, as a last-ditch effort (my cousin was never one to give up easily), he bought tickets for a sold-out concert that he knew she'd want to go to. According to Travis, *all* women loved Julio Iglesias.

When he showed up at her apartment door and presented her with the tickets, she threatened to call the police if he didn't leave. If she'd just give him a chance, she'd see that he wasn't a bad guy, Travis had told her. But she kept threatening to call the police. That was just lip service, he'd told me. He knew that he had broken through to her because she had been making that threat for ten minutes and hadn't once moved toward picking up the telephone. It was when she started screaming that sent Travis over the edge. All he wanted was for her to just give him a chance. He had never *planned* to rape her, and killing her was definitely a mistake, he'd admitted.

And that's just what his lawyer argued when Travis's day in court came. But that's not how a jury of seven men and five women saw it. Nor was it the way the judge or the prosecutor saw it. When Travis was sentenced to life in prison, the woman's brother, who was locked up for killing a man and his entire family—on purpose—didn't see it that way either.

Like I said, Travis was mean and bad, but I think something deep down inside of who he was changed, especially after that butt whipping Daddy gave him that summer of the family reunion. I think Daddy always felt guilty about whipping Travis the way he did. And Daddy hardly ever felt guilty about anything. I'm sure he didn't feel guilty about pulling a gun on Mr. Banister, who lived down the street from us on East 105th and Quincy Avenue, where I grew up.

It was around three o'clock early one Saturday morning when I was awakened from a beautiful dream I was having about Marcus Hilton, the thirteen-year-old love of my dreams. I heard all this shouting and cussing, which wasn't all that unusual. Since Daddy wasn't exactly a churchgoing man, the fact that he was going off on somebody was neither shocking nor new. What was new, though, was the way Daddy *sounded* while he was going off. He sounded so angry, so hard.

I hopped out of my bed, stretched my small body out onto the hardwood floor, and pressed my ear to the floor so I could hear what was going on. Mama was crying and begging Daddy to put the gun away, saying that it was only a card game. And Ms. Inez, Mr. Banister's girlfriend, was pleading with Mr. Banister to "just let them have the book!" Later on I found out they had been playing bid whist.

I could tell by the way my Daddy's speech slurred slightly that he was drunk when he said, "I'm gon' put a bullet so far up in you that even God won't be able to find it!" Mama kept telling

Daddy that if he didn't calm down, he was going to have a heart attack, what with his bad heart and all. Daddy kept right on yelling and acting a fool, not paying Mama any attention whatsoever. After what seemed like hours, Mama was finally able to calm Daddy down and get him to go to bed.

Seems all Mama ever did was calm Daddy down. She was the most dedicated wife I've ever known. A little too dedicated. Staying with a man because she loved him was one thing, but staying with a man because she felt she had no place else to go was something entirely different. And pitiful.

I remember the shock and sadness I felt after walking in on what obviously was supposed to be a private moment between spouses. Having gone unheard by my parents, I stood perfectly still, holding my breath, as I witnessed my mother's unconscionable behavior. My mother, "the fragile flower," as I had nicknamed her, was kneeling at my father's side, his feet in her hands, as he sat in a folding chair in the middle of the living room. She had the big, white family Bible that usually sat on the cocktail table in the living room open to the 23rd Psalm, lying on the floor in front of her while she read from one of the Gospel accounts. As she read, she enacted the event that had taken place. Only it wasn't her tears that wet his feet; it was water that she lapped like a dog from a basin on the floor beside her. She would let the water from her mouth drizzle onto my father's feet, and then she would wipe his feet with her hair. The oil she used was not perfumed oil but olive oil. After she had rubbed his feet with it, she proceeded to lick the oil off with her tongue and cover his feet with her kisses. Something in my young mind told me that this was not normal, and that's when I perceived my "fragile flower" had begun to lose some of its petals.

Mama was a beautiful woman inside and out. The problem was that, like so many women in abusive relationships, she didn't know it. Daddy told her over and over that she wouldn't be able to make it in this world without him until Mama believed him. Hadn't he always provided for her, let her stay at home and raise the kids, and taken care of her and the kids? Had he ever brought his women to the house? Hadn't he been good to her? I can remember Daddy throwing those words at Mama throughout my childhood whenever she broached the subject of taking a class at the community college. She didn't need some old fool white man professor poisoning her mind, he'd say. Her job and responsibility was to her husband and children.

Mama gave her life to my Daddy. I wonder sometimes if she ever regretted it. I think she did. When she didn't know I was watching, I'd see a look of impatience or longing, maybe even regret, come onto Mama's face. Looked to me like she was struggling with whether or not to let the expression stay or go. She should have let it stay; it would have served as a reminder of all she'd lost by staying with Daddy. Maybe then she would have found the courage to find herself and move on.

Life is peculiar in a way. Many times I've wondered why and how I managed to escape the madness that seemed to touch my family. I don't know the answer to that question. What I do know is that in my forty-two years, I've come to learn that no matter where we begin, we can never know where—or when, for that matter—we'll end up.

Some days, like today, when I have time between patients, I stare at the PhD behind my name on the degree hanging on my wall and think of my family—Grandma Beasley, whose freedom from the Ohio Reformatory for Women finally did come the day she took her last breath; Joshua, who, not able to bear the guilt of knowing what he'd done to an innocent family, hanged himself; Travis, who some might say got what was coming to him when the woman's brother raped and killed him in prison; Daddy, whose heart finally did give out; and Mama, who, though still breathing, is dead inside—and get to missing them.

By no definition were we a perfect family. If I had my way, I'd have been the sixth child of Clair and Heathcliff Huxtable. But my life was more than a twenty-two-minute, one-day-a-week television show, and despite our imperfections, we loved each other, faults and all. I believe that's what family should do. That's why, every chance I get, I tell people, "We may not be able to choose our families, but we can choose to love them."

And that's the truth.

THINK AGAIN

CASHMERE HURRIEDLY TURNED THE KEY IN THE LOCK, SWUNG open the door, dropped her backpack and purse on the floor, and raced to the bathroom. Just in time, she made it, swinging her head over the sink as another wave of nausea washed over her. This was the fifth straight day she'd gotten sick for no apparent reason, always in her 8:50 a.m. statistics class.

She rinsed her mouth with warm water and wiped her face with a cold washcloth, then peered at her reflection in the mirror. Cashmere frowned at the bags that were beginning to form under her eyes. She was only twenty-two, too young to have puffy eyes. First the nausea, now the eyes. What was happening to her? *Must be pre-wedding jitters*, she thought.

Everything seemed to be unraveling, and she felt so out of control. If there was one thing Cashmere didn't like, it was not being in control. *Why can't professionals act professional?* she pondered. Only two weeks before the wedding, and the band hadn't confirmed yet. Her maid of honor had to be refitted for her dress, and it wasn't even ready yet. She should have just told her to go pick a dress off the rack at David's Bridal in Cleveland instead of coming all the way to Rochester to have Raymond's mother make the dress.

Even as she thought it, Cashmere knew that was out of the question. This was her wedding, and she wouldn't have anyone in her bridal party wearing off-the-rack specials. In addition to having to deal with the issue of the dress and the terrible headache that was pounding at her temples, Cashmere noticed that Raymond's temper seemed to be getting shorter and shorter lately. Everything she did was either too much this or not enough that. He was getting on her last nerve; couldn't he see that she was doing the best she could? He was the one who had wanted to push the wedding date up by almost a year. Cashmere had only agreed to it because he was so persuasive. *Persuasive and fine*, she thought. Cashmere couldn't say no to a man with dimples as deep as his and a smile that turned her to butter. His smile was what had initially attracted her to him. Cashmere leaned against the sink, thinking of the man with whom she would grow old.

She was nineteen when she met Raymond, but she knew all those months ago that he was the one for her. If she was nothing else, Cashmere was a good judge of character, and she prided herself on that. It wasn't long after they'd started dating that she moved out of the dorm she shared with two other freshmen and into Raymond's three-bedroom, ranch-style home.

Raymond, fifteen years her senior, was worldly wise. He taught her things about life that only someone who had lived it would know. He introduced her to a world that was foreign to her, one she hoped to be a part of when she graduated from college. Cashmere considered herself lucky to have met a man who not only shared her interest in computers but worked for a Fortune 500 computer company. He was her "in" into the world of computer technology. Raymond had all but promised Cashmere a job with the company he worked for once she graduated college with a double major in computer science and graphic arts.

The only downside to their relationship was that Raymond's job sent him out of town at least once a month for conventions, but he'd promised to take her with him sometime to give her more exposure. In the meantime, he took her to every social function his job sponsored. Raymond paraded Cashmere in front of the CEOs of major corporations, letting her observe him in his element, teaching her the language of the trade, and encouraging her to mingle and talk shop with the big boys. Ever the overachiever, Cashmere had followed Raymond's lead to perfection.

"Tiny," Raymond had said on one such occasion, using the pet name he had given her not long after they had started going out. "Let's go over this one more time. I don't want you to embarrass yourself at the table." The table Raymond was referring to was a dinner table at a $750-a-plate affair for the Rochester NAACP, an annual fund-raiser gala benefiting underprivileged youth.

"On what side are your drinking glasses?" Raymond had asked.

"Right."

"Eating utensils?"

"Forks on the left. Knives and spoons on the right."

"What about the napkin?"

"Unfold it and place it in my lap. Use it only to dab my lips or wipe my fingers. Don't rub my hands with it; 'it's not a washcloth, for Christ's sake!' And never, never, *never* ball it up and throw it on the table! When I'm done, I should place it neatly on the dinner plate." Cashmere flashed Raymond a playful grin. "So, how did I do, teacher?"

"This isn't a joking matter, Cashmere. All the important people from my job will be there, and I want you to make a good impression. I want them to see that you're cultured; that you're not just some fresh-eyed young girl from around the way. What you do and how you behave is a reflection on me. Got it?"

Raymond could be so uptight about things at times, Cashmere remembered thinking. This was their first social event as a couple, and he had been obsessing about it for the last three weeks. She had reassured him that he had nothing to worry about it, but it was like talking to the wind. "I got it," Cashmere said between half-clenched teeth.

"I'm going to take a shower," Raymond announced.

"Wait! You need to help me decide which dress to wear." Nobody, male or female, could put together an ensemble the way Raymond could. When she'd met him, her wardrobe had consisted exclusively of T-shirts and jeans. Not long after, she traded in her jeans for front-pleated dress slacks and A-line skirts and her T-shirts for blouses and sweaters. She loved learning fashion sense and social etiquette from Raymond.

For the briefest moment, Cashmere thought she detected a glint of annoyance in Raymond's eyes. "I thought we had decided on the teal Dior dress and the silver Via Spiga sandals," Raymond said, heading toward their bedroom with Cashmere on his heels.

"We did. But I tried it on yesterday and it's a little tight."

"Tight?" Panic rose in Raymond's voice. "I told you to lay off all that chocolate." His reply had come out gruff, so unlike the persona he projected. He opened the closet door and sorted through the dresses. Picking out several, he tossed them on the bed. Then he sorted through the shoes hanging on the over-the-door rack, matched up shoes with dresses, and told Cashmere to try on the ensembles.

Four hours later they emerged, the perfectly matched pair: he wearing a navy Armani double-breasted suit with Allen Edmonds walnut cap-toe shoes, and she wearing a chocolate Diane von Furstenberg evening dress, with tan Stuart Weitzman peep-toe pumps and a matching handbag.

The night had gone off flawlessly.

Raymond was big on sophistication and comportment. He believed that a woman should carry herself with dignity and graciousness, always. He also believed that what a person chose to wear dictated their behavior and ultimately how they felt about themselves. That's why he had insisted on swathing Cashmere in the latest designer clothes and keeping a standing weekly hair, manicure, and pedicure appointment.

"Any woman of mine has to be cultured," Raymond had said, shortly after they'd started dating. So once a month he taught Cashmere facts about foreign countries and bought her expensive gifts native to those countries, creating in her a desire to visit parts of the world she had never imagined visiting, places she had only seen or read about in travel brochures. Cashmere wanted that life. Ever since she was a child, she had fantasized about a life without so many financial restrictions. Growing up as an only child in the low-income areas of Cleveland, Ohio, Cashmere had promised herself that she would do whatever it took to make sure that her life as an adult would be much better than the life she had as a child. That's why she had so readily accepted Raymond's proposal of marriage eighteen months after they had started dating.

On a languid, breezy morning on spring break in Cancun, with the Mexican sun a beautiful burnt sienna, Cashmere and Raymond were wrapped in each other's embrace when Raymond had popped the question.

"I've never loved *anyone* as much as I love you, Tiny. You are so very pertinent to my life, my very being. Your unfailing love and devotion has helped me appreciate what it means to be a man, through and through. With this ring, I give you my guarantee that as long as I have breath in my lungs, no harm will ever befall you."

Thinking about that splendid proposal gave Cashmere goose bumps. She turned her hand this way and that, openly admiring the three-carat diamond on her left ring finger. She took the engagement ring off and read the inscription: "For my jewel. 4ever, Ray." The promise ring she had given Raymond was cut glass compared to her ring, but he didn't care. He showed it off to everyone he knew.

Cashmere was sidetracked on her way to her bedroom to lie down. In the far corner of the living room, Raymond's secretary drew Cashmere's attention. She saw a key chain with several keys on it lying on the desktop. The unguarded keys were a peculiar sight because Raymond never left the keys to his desk lying around. He must have come home while she was in the bathroom.

"Ray! Ray!" Cashmere called out. No answer. She went to the stair landing and called his name again. Again, no answer. "Hmm. . . . That's weird," she said, going back into the living room. She looked suspiciously at the secretary, undecided as to what to do, as if she had to *do* anything.

Raymond was always so secretive about what he kept in the desk. When she'd asked him why he kept it locked, he'd said that's where he kept his important papers, and in case someone broke in, he didn't want them to be able to get at them too easily. She let him believe that she bought his tale, but she couldn't help being curious. It wasn't that she didn't trust Raymond; she trusted him with her life. It was just that she believed that couples, especially a couple as close as they were, should be open about everything. That's why after he'd told her that, she went looking for the keys, to no avail. And now here they were, just begging her to take a look inside.

She tried every key until the lock on the center drawer, beneath the desktop, finally gave. Papers were neatly stacked inside the old-fashioned cherry wood secretary typical Raymond style: envelopes were stacked in a neat pile separately from the papers according to size, with the larger envelopes on the bottom. She reached in and pulled out a large envelope. Opening it, she found that it contained the deed to the house, stock and bond certificates, and financial statements. Nothing she didn't already know about. She wondered if this was what Raymond meant by "important papers." *Some men*, she thought. *Anything to make themselves look important.*

She was about to close the drawer when something—she didn't know what—compelled her to pull the drawer all the way out. She did, but there was nothing in back of the drawer or behind it. Cashmere shut the drawer and snatched the keys off the desk, anxious to get it locked again in case Raymond suddenly showed up. A noise from outside caused Cashmere to drop the keys. The scuffling sound told her that it was only a squirrel. When she bent to pick up the keys, she noticed something hanging out of a slit in the back of one of the drawers. She yanked the object but it wouldn't budge. A slamming car door halted her efforts, and she quickly placed the keys back on the desk the way she'd found them. Her heart pounded furiously as she moved rapidly from the living room to the front door.

"What are you doing home so early?" Raymond asked, coming through the door. He looked suspiciously at Cashmere.

"I could ask you the same thing," Cashmere said in lieu of an answer. She hoped the shock of his sudden appearance wasn't evident on her face.

"My client was just fifteen minutes away, so I thought I'd come home for lunch. Since you're here, how about we make this a lunch date?" He moved in close to Cashmere and kissed her on the neck. "Mmm . . ." he said, snuggling a little closer. "I always love the way Boucheron smells on you."

"I wish I could eat something, but my stomach's been upset lately. That's why I'm home. I just need to lie down. All the stress of planning the wedding is catching up with me." She stepped out of Raymond's embrace and grabbed his hand, swinging it the way a small child would when holding onto an adult. Far from being an act of childish behavior, this odd act worked as a calming tactic for Raymond, Cashmere had discovered. She needed him to be calm. Ray had told her from the beginning not to try to handle the details by herself and that she should hire a wedding planner, but she had insisted on doing everything herself. Admitting that the planning was overwhelming her would upset Ray, and she wanted to stop his anger before it could surface.

Raymond pulled his hand from Cashmere's grasp. "Let's get out of this vestibule," he said, heading for the kitchen. "Come sit with me while I make myself something to eat. You can tell me all about your problems, and I promise I won't say I told you so."

The last thing Cashmere wanted to do was sit around and talk—her head still pounded and the queasiness hadn't completely gone away. But she obliged, grateful to have averted a potential tirade. As Raymond prepared his lunch, Cashmere sat at the kitchen table and filled him in on where things stood with the wedding and reception preparations.

"Don't worry about that," Raymond said, when she told him about the trouble with the DJ, cutting his turkey sandwich in half. He spread a linen napkin across his lap to protect his pants. "I'll deal with that when I get home this evening."

No matter how often Cashmere observed Raymond's table manners, it was something she didn't think she would ever get used to. Most men she'd known were brutes; a shirtsleeve was the closest they'd come to using a napkin.

"Oh, before I forget. Jorgé called about the insurance policy. He wants you to call him." At the mention of his insurance agent, Raymond's expression changed. "What's the matter?" Cashmere asked, concerned.

"Nothing. I was just wondering why he called the house and not the office or my cell." He bit into his sandwich and chewed slowly.

"He did try the office. He said he left you a voice mail, but he thought he would try you at home just in case you hadn't gone in today. And he said your cell went straight to voice mail and there's a message there also. It's just a simple beneficiary change; what's so urgent that he's touching all the bases?"

"That's what I'm wondering. Anyway, I'll call him when I get back to the office." Raymond finished his sandwich and drank down the last of his green tea. He glanced at the clock on the wall and proclaimed he had to hurry back for a 1:30 meeting.

On his way out, Raymond stopped abruptly. "My keys," he said, going toward the secretary. "I was wondering where I had put them. Did you know these were here?" Raymond asked suspiciously, pointing at the keys.

Cashmere made her expression impassive. "I saw them there earlier. Why?"

"I had been looking for them, that's all." He pocketed the keys. "I've got to go. I'll see you when I get home tonight."

Alone in the house once again and determined to find out what the mystery object was, Cashmere went back to the secretary to try to retrieve what was stuck between the side board and the back of the top drawer. She pulled and yanked, pushed and tugged until finally the object came loose. It turned out to be a tan, business-sized envelope with no identifying information written on the outside. It was unsealed, the flap tucked neatly inside. Cashmere lifted the flap and carefully took out the contents. Photographs. Two of them. In one photograph stood Raymond next to his workmate Audra in business attire, with an exquisite-looking man who looked to be of Asian descent, casually dressed. They all had wide grins plastered across their faces. The other photograph was of the same exquisite-looking man with Audra, who was holding the hand of a small child who looked to be around two or three years old.

Cashmere flipped the photographs over and studied the captions on the back. The first photo was dated almost four years ago and captioned in perfect penmanship "Seattle, WA, HP convention, Ray, Audra & Jerrold." On the other picture was written, "Audra, Jerrold and little M (2.5 years)." The child resembled neither Audra nor the man, and Cashmere wondered if in fact the couple had adopted the child from some impoverished country. *Good for them*, Cashmere thought. When she and Raymond got settled in their marriage, maybe they would consider adopting a child from a third world country. When they started dating, Raymond had made it clear that while he loved children, he didn't want any of his own. He told Cashmere that there were too many children in need of a loving home and that if he felt the stirrings of fatherhood, then he'd satisfy his desire by adopting one of them. Cashmere, having come from a broken family and feeling no desire to give birth, had agreed with Raymond.

Her curiosity satisfied, Cashmere placed the photographs back into the envelope and shoved the envelope back where she'd gotten it. She hoped and prayed that Raymond would never know that she had gone snooping in his desk drawers. He would be devastated to know that she hadn't believed his explanation of the contents of his desk.

***

The warbler ringtone emanating from the bedside table startled Cashmere awake. Groggy from sleep, she snatched up the telephone. "Hello," she said huskily into the receiver. No response. She repeated her greeting several times before finally giving up and hanging up. She checked the caller ID. The call had come from a restricted number. *Must be a wrong number.* Cashmere squinted at the small numbers on her wristwatch: 2:45. She had been asleep for almost ninety minutes. She eased out of bed, stretched, yawned, and had begun making the bed when a thought occurred to her. She hadn't heard from Mrs. Lesure, Raymond's mother, about the maid of honor's refitting. She dialed the familiar number.

After receiving a reassuring report from her future mother-in-law, Cashmere hung up the phone, ready to tackle more items on her seemingly insurmountable pre-wedding to-do list. She punched in the number of the caterer and was about to hit the send button when the phone rang. "Restricted" again. Cashmere answered the telephone ready to do battle. But it was only her sorority sister Lisa calling to give Cashmere her assignment for the annual Red Cross blood drive.

"Lisa, I have too much going on right now. You know my wedding is in two weeks and we have the bridal party luncheon next Saturday. Can you get someone else?" Cashmere asked the question with trepidation. She knew that refusing an assignment could cost her popularity points, not to mention have other repercussions.

"Can't do that. Everybody who volunteered has already been given assignments. You're the last person on the list. Anyway, I made sure you had the easiest assignment, since I know you don't have a lot of extra time. Look, all you have to do is find at least fifty people to donate blood and that's it. You can start with your fiancé."

"That takes care of one person," Cashmere sighed. "Now all I have to do is find forty-nine more. The timing for this thing really sucks!" she protested.

After talking about strategies for finding donors, Cashmere ended the conversation and allowed herself to momentarily be distracted from wedding plans as she placed call after call to friends, family members, acquaintances, and random numbers from the White pages. One hour later, she had acquired fifteen yeses, eight maybes, and more noes than she cared to admit.

"Why are you sitting there with your lips poked out?" Raymond asked, shrugging out of his suit jacket as he entered the bedroom. He folded the jacket and laid it across the bed.

Cashmere jumped, startled. She was so preoccupied with her thoughts that she hadn't seen or heard Raymond come in. In answer to his question, she told Raymond all about the blood drive she had forgotten that she'd volunteered for. "So counting you, I've got sixteen yeses."

Raymond abruptly turned away, but not before Cashmere noticed his alarmed expression. "What's with the look?" Cashmere asked.

Raymond remained silent and continued undressing. He took his robe from where it hung on the inside of the closet door and put it on.

"Oh, no," Cashmere said and began laughing. "Don't tell me. You're afraid of needles, aren't you?" She stood beside him and stroked his bicep. "Seriously," she said, "there's nothing to it. I'll be right there with you. I won't let that big bad needle hurt you," she said playfully.

Raymond ignored the laughter and gently removed Cashmere's hand from his arm. "It's not that," he said. Reluctantly, he turned to face her. "I need to tell you something."

From outside, the pounding bass of a car stereo at full blast could be heard as it sped down the small side street. Despite the numerous signs posted, motorists continued to use their little street as a shortcut to the main road. Raymond had said the tranquility of the neighborhood was what had attracted him to the area, but it was the peace he felt coming home that kept him there. At this moment, Raymond looked to Cashmere to be anything but a man at peace.

"Let's sit down," Raymond said. "Can we sit down? Let's sit on the bed." He was saying things in threes. That's what he did when he got nervous. That was the one tell that Raymond couldn't hide.

Cashmere sat with Raymond on the bed. She took his hands in hers and gently swung them back and forth until, pressing her thumb to the vein in his wrist, she could feel his pulse become steady. "Like you tell me all the time, Ray, 'don't over-think it, just put it out there.'" Cashmere didn't honestly know if she was ready to hear what Raymond had to tell her. But she couldn't remain in this animated state of expectation. If just the thought of having this conversation was causing Raymond so severe a reaction, she imagined that hearing what he had to say just might kill her. She scolded herself for being so dramatic.

"This was before I met you," Raymond began. Before he could finish his speech, the tears were pouring from his eyes and he was crying audibly.

Cashmere sat quietly, her stomach in knots, her own heart beating erratically. She had never seen a man cry. Part of her was repulsed at the sight of this man whom she considered a tower of strength sitting there helplessly, shamefully raw with emotion. The other part of her, the more compassionate, humane part was so filled with pity and love for him that she wanted to carry the burden of whatever sin he was trying to confess.

Cashmere pulled Raymond to her and stroked the back of his head and his neck, whispering to him over and over, "It's okay. It's okay."

In the long yawn of silence, they held each other. After a while, Raymond went to the bathroom, wet a towel, and ran it across his face. Embarrassed by his display of emotion, he couldn't bring himself to face Cashmere. He stood rather than sat. Humiliated, he looked down at his feet. "I'm sorry," he mumbled.

Not knowing what to say, Cashmere smiled weakly. As the minutes ticked by, she became more aware of how uncomfortably thick the air between them had become. "Ray, you're scaring me," she whispered. "What is it you want me to know?" She wanted to run and hide; she didn't know how to respond to his display of emotion. "Just spit it out!" she wanted to scream, but she couldn't be that insensitive.

"Before I met you, I had a friend that I was close to. We were roommates. I got transferred from the Seattle office to here. That's where I met Audra, in Washington —"

"Are you trying to tell me that you and Audra used to live together?" Cashmere cut in.

"No. That's not what I'm saying. There's never been anything between Audra and me. She's my workmate and a close friend, nothing more. I'm just saying that I knew Audra when I lived in Washington."

"But you told me that before. And it's not a big deal that you used to live with someone. I wasn't a virgin myself when I met you."

"No. That's not what I'm saying. You need to just listen." Exasperation was evident in his voice. Raymond hated when Cashmere interrupted him; it was a bad habit of hers, and he was becoming more agitated each time she cut him off. He sat down in the wingback chair in the corner of the room and put his elbows on his knees, rubbing his head with both hands as he visibly contemplated getting through his story without disruption.

"For real, Ray," Cashmere said, reading Raymond's expression. "That's old news. It happened before you and I got together, and there's no need for you to feel like you have to confess your past to me. I forgive you, all right? Now stop tripping about it. God! People say *women* are drama queens!" Cashmere got up from the bed and headed for the living room. She wanted to unwind before getting started on a homework assignment for her C# programming class.

"I had a romantic relationship with a man before I met you!" Raymond blurted out.

Cashmere froze where she stood. Had she heard him correctly? The pounding in her head threatened to drop her to her knees, but she couldn't move. The queasiness that had brought her home from school early today had returned, and the bile at the back of her throat was working its way upward. She had to get a grip. Blackness was only moments away; she felt as if she would faint any minute now. She willed herself to put one foot in front of the other, but nothing happened. Her synapses weren't firing in sync. She could feel Raymond's eyes boring into her back, waiting for a response. When she opened her mouth to respond, nothing came out. She felt, rather than heard, Raymond come up behind her. His voice, when he spoke, sounded tinny and muffled. What was happening to her? She must be in shock, she concluded. When at last she was able to move, she turned and faced Raymond, a look of repulsion clouding her otherwise pretty features.

Raymond reached out to take Cashmere's elbow to lead her back into the bedroom and she flinched, snatching her arm away violently. "Don't touch me!" she hissed through clenched teeth.

"Please, Cashmere, don't shut me out," Raymond begged. "I promise you that was before I met you. We had already been broken up a year at the time you and I started going out. Can we at least talk about it?"

"Oh my God! *Oh my God!* This is *not* happening to me! It's not!" she screamed. "You're a liar, Ray. I should have seen it. I should have known it! You're too pretty; too perfect. Seriously, what man gives a damn about what fork a person uses, or what they talk about at the dinner table, or whether a napkin is used and especially how it's placed on the table at the end of the meal? And why do you know so much about clothes, especially women's clothes? It was right there in front of my face and I didn't see it. Why are you telling me this now? Why are you telling me at all? You went this long, why now?" Through her rage, Cashmere felt an overwhelming sense of sadness begin to grow within her. Although she asked the questions, nothing Raymond did or said would make her forgive his betrayal. Their life together was a lie. He wasn't the man he purported to be.

Cashmere faced Raymond and saw that the tears were back. She was too angry to feel anything for him but disgust.

Raymond backed away from Cashmere and looked away. "I'm sorry," he choked out. "I didn't want us to start our marriage off on a lie. I've wanted to tell you for a long time, but I didn't know how." He wiped his eyes with the back of his hands and let out a moan. "Please don't leave me, Cashmere," Raymond begged. "I love you so much. Don't leave me!"

"You love me? Yeah, right." The statement dripped with sarcasm. "Tell me something, Ray. How long did the 'relationship' last?" The pain in her head along with the queasiness in her stomach had subsided a little, and she was starting to feel calmer.

"It wasn't long; a little over a year. We lived together for three months, I swear. He wasn't right for me. I had never been in that type of relationship. It just didn't feel right." He breathed out a long, deep sigh of relief, as if in the telling he had found absolution.

"What do you mean 'it didn't feel right'? Are you or are you not gay, Ray?"

"I can't explain what I mean. I just didn't feel comfortable, with us living together. And I'm definitely not gay! I admit I like men, but I like women, too."

"So you're saying you're bi?"

He took longer than Cashmere thought was necessary to answer. "If you have to put a name on it, then yes, I guess some people would call it that. Personally, I don't think labels are necessary. I promise you, Cash, you don't have anything to worry about. I'm with you now and I'm completely devoted."

"How do I know that? Really. How do I know that your ex-boyfriend won't show up on our doorstep looking to get something going with you again?" Cashmere shook her head, still unable to believe that she was actually sitting in her bedroom, two weeks before her wedding, having this type of conversation with her fiancé. The total shock of it hadn't worn off yet. She didn't think it ever would.

"You know because I'm promising you that it won't. Besides, he's already tried to start it up with me again and I flat-out told him no."

"You what? You mean to tell me that you've been in touch with this man while we were together?"

"No," he said adamantly. "He contacted me. He called work months ago when he heard that I was getting married." Raymond raised his hand in the stop motion to prevent Cashmere from interjecting a comment. "I didn't tell him about the engagement, Audra did. They were friends long before he and I met."

At the mention of Audra's name, Cashmere grew suspicious, thinking of the photo she had found in Raymond's secretary. "Who is this man, Ray? What's his name?" she asked anxiously.

"It's over between us; his name isn't important. You don't know him, trust me."

"I want to know his name, Ray," Cashmere protested.

"Tell me how knowing his name would change the facts or make a difference," Raymond demanded.

"It would show me that you're willing to be completely open and honest with me."

Raymond pondered the statement, then on a sigh said, "His name is Robert."

"Does this Robert have a last name?" Cashmere pushed.

"He does, but I won't tell you that. He's not out and I'm not going to be the one to out him. Besides Audra, you're the only one who knows about our relationship. As far as everyone else knew, I was a cousin who needed a place to stay after his girlfriend kicked him out. Anyway, this is about me, not him. Like I said, Cash, what we had is over. I'm no longer interested in him or that lifestyle. You're the woman I want to spend the rest of my life with."

Cashmere couldn't come up with a convincing argument for why Raymond should divulge Robert's last name, so she let the question go unanswered. She felt a knot form in her throat and tears tease the corners of her eyes. She hadn't cried since she was eleven years old, when her Nana had died, and she wouldn't cry now. After her parents divorced, Nana was the one person Cashmere felt loved her unconditionally and unquestioningly. Sunday afternoons after church, she would go to her Nana's house, and her Nana would teach her how to cook, dispense wisdom to her, and regale her with stories of the "olden days." If ever Cashmere needed the wisdom of her Nana, it was now. *What should I do, Nana?* Cashmere said in her heart. She imagined hearing the mellifluous sound of her Nana's deep voice saying to her, "Chile, you know that God forgives all hearts. If you can love and live with this man knowing what you know, follow your heart and God will take care of the rest."

"I can't be here right now," Cashmere said. "I'm going out." She rose from the bed and walked out of the room, stopping only long enough to open the front the door and walk through it. She ignored Raymond's inquires about whether she was coming back.

***

Two days later when Cashmere stood on the porch of the home she shared with Raymond, she had made up her mind what she was going to do. On the night she left, she hadn't asked the most important question—not because she had forgotten to, but because knowing the answer would have been too emotionally taxing. Having been blindsided by Raymond's confession, she didn't think she could handle knowing one more thing, irrespective of the answer. She would ask today. And the answer would decide their future.

She had spent the last two days in Cleveland at the home of her maid of honor. Cashmere had confided everything to her. When she finished talking, Annette had asked her only two questions: "Has he been tested for HIV, and do you still want to be with him?"

"Okay, the first question I understand," Cashmere had said. "But what does the second question have to do with anything?"

Annette had looked at Cashmere as though she had grown a second head. "Because if you still wanna be with him, then girl, the only thing that's keeping you at my house is not knowing his HIV status."

Driving back to Rochester, New York, Cashmere had mulled over the conversation in her mind. She had to admit that Annette's reasoning, though a little flawed, did make some sense. The thought of being with Raymond intimately hadn't crossed Cashmere's mind. Not because she didn't want him or desire him, but she was still having trouble coming to grips with his revelation. She loved Raymond, she knew that. Her feelings for him had never been in question. She was feeling hurt, even devastated. She would get over it; she would have to because even now, knowing what she did, she wanted a life with Raymond. He had opened up to her a world that she was anxious to be a part of permanently. She had known that she couldn't stay hidden away at Annette's house indefinitely. After allowing her two days of isolation and reflection, Annette had packed Cashmere into her old Honda and sent her home.

Cashmere opened the front door and took a deep breath. She walked toward the sound of the television coming from the spare bedroom that Raymond had turned into an office. She knocked lightly and he looked up. The smile he exhibited was tinged with uncertainty. He shut off the television and rose from his chair to stand tentatively beside Cashmere.

Cashmere's lack of retreat seemed to indicate to Raymond that all was well. He made a move to embrace her, but she recoiled.

"What's your status, Ray?" she said without preamble.

"My wh—? Oh . . ." He said, realizing what she was asking. "I'm negative. I got tested six months after Robert and I broke up. I can show you the test results." Raymond retrieved his laptop from his desk and typed in the Web address to his health insurance carrier. He logged in and typed a range of dates, then waited for the page to load. Walking back to where Cashmere stood, he held the laptop out so that she could read the screen. He pointed to a line that said, "HIV antibodies—negative."

Tremendous relief washed over Cashmere. She exhaled air that she was unaware she had been holding. She lowered herself onto the floor and sat cross-legged, hugging her knees close to her chest. Raymond put the laptop down and joined Cashmere on the floor.

"I have my whole life ahead of me, Ray. My parents divorced when I was young, and I promised myself I would never marry someone who didn't love me. I feel like you took a knife and cut my heart right out of my chest. What am I supposed to do with what you told me? I feel so hollow, so empty," Cashmere whispered, almost completely drained of energy.

"You file it away as something that happened in the past, before we met. And you trust me when I say to you that I love *you*. I want to be with *you*. There's no one in this world that I want to spend the rest of my life with but *you, Cashmere*. I don't know how to make you believe that; only time and trust will show you."

Cashmere stared out the window at the huge oak tree on the neighboring front lawn. The branches stretched beyond the driveway to just where Raymond's property line began. At nine, she had fallen out of a tree just like it in the backyard of her childhood home. Her mother had scolded her about climbing the tree, warning that Cashmere could hurt herself or even die if she didn't stop monkeying around on the tree. The excruciating pain that had shot through her arm when her body had made contact with the ground after falling ten feet was nothing compared to what she was now feeling.

"Say we're married for a few weeks, months, years, whatever, and you get the urge to phone up this Robert, or he calls you— what then? How do I compete with that? Obviously I can't give you what he can." Her brown eyes searched his for consolation. His expression was difficult to read. Raymond ran his hand across the neatly trimmed hairs that almost entirely covered his top lip, then fingered the soul patch beneath his bottom lip. The gesture was one that Cashmere had seen Raymond perform many times when he was trying to find a way to explain a difficult concept, especially when it related to computer programming.

Raymond eased his slight frame from where he was sitting and went to stand by the window. His gaze turned toward the wailing sirens that could be heard in the distance. Fire trucks. The faint smell of smoke wafted in through the hidden crevices of the house. When he turned to face Cashmere, Raymond's expression was as unreadable as Cashmere had ever seen it.

"You don't compete, Cash. All right? You just don't." He sighed. "Look," he said, leaning his back against the wall. "You're asking me to foretell the future. I can't do that. I've told you what my intentions are; that's the best I can do. If you need more time to digest all this, I'll understand. If you want to postpone the wedding, I'll even understand that. And if you don't want to marry me, I'll understand that too. I know I dropped a bomb on you, but I thought you deserved to know the truth."

Raymond was right: she was asking him to do the impossible. He had a clean bill of health, and he'd broken it off with the guy long before they had met. Raymond was devoted to her; she knew that. When they were together, she was the focus of his attention. Although he could be controlling and overbearing sometimes, he had never been deceitful.

"I know what you're saying is right, Ray. I don't need more time to think about anything. I want to go ahead with the wedding. It's like you said: all of that happened . . ." A low humming sound emanated from Raymond, interrupting the conversation.

Raymond glanced down at the phone strapped to his belt, then back up to Cashmere. "Do you mind?" he asked, a look of annoyance crossing his face. "It's Jorgé, getting back to me about the insurance policy."

She waved a dismissive hand at Raymond. "Go ahead. I'm tired of talking anyway," she said. Cashmere extricated herself from her sitting position on the floor and left Raymond to his conversation. As she exited the room, she heard the catch in Raymond's voice when he said, "So now what do I do?"

"Everything okay?" Cashmere asked as Raymond joined her in the living room, having finished his business.

"Yeah. It's good. Everything is fine."

He was doing that threesome thing again, so Cashmere pushed. "You were able to change the beneficiary?"

"Oh, yeah." He rubbed the back of his neck and raked his nails over his scalp.

"It's just that you sounded worried when I left the room."

"Yeah. Oh, that was nothing. I wanted to increase the policy. Jorgé advised against it for now and said I should wait until after we're married since the insurance company requires a physical exam for anything past $500,000, even though I already have a policy with them. He knows the wedding is in a few days and we're limited on time. That's all. Hey, how about we get Chinese take-out tonight? I can pick it up since I need to make a run to CVS anyway."

He was talking at the speed of light, but Cashmere detected that there was something not quite right with Raymond's explanation. She was too spent to make further inquiries, so she agreed to have Chinese.

"You make the call and I'll see you in thirty," Raymond said, heading out the door.

***

The night before the wedding, not a problem was in sight. Raymond had been right to hire a wedding planner at the last minute. Cheryll Howell was a godsend. She had stepped in and handled the last-minute details with military precision. The church and reception hall were all decorated and just waiting for tomorrow. The rehearsal dinner went off without a hitch. The only small inconvenience was that her maid of honor, Annette, wasn't able to make it, but thankfully, Raymond was able to talk Audra into acting as a surrogate.

After the rehearsal dinner the groomsmen, best man, male relatives, and ushers had taken Raymond to a location that no one was willing to disclose to Cashmere for a "last celebratory night of freedom." Cashmere hadn't minded; her sorority sisters were throwing her a private party at Hunkalicious on Henrietta Road, which was where her Zeta sisters, the bridal party, and other invited guests now sat whooping and hollering words of encouragement to the buffed men, who came in all colors of the rainbow, occupying the stage.

Although she wasn't an official member of the bridal party, Audra had accepted Lisa's invitation to join the celebration. Several drinks in, Cashmere noticed that Audra's speech was beginning to slur and she had loosened up considerably. At the rehearsal she had been wound so tight that Cashmere could barely get six words out of her. She had probably never been in a setting where she was considered the minority. Appletinis were definitely just what the doctor had ordered to get Audra to relax.

"Cashmere!" Audra yelled over the loud music, swaying a bit before flopping down in the chair opposite Cashmere. "I want to congratulate you on your upcoming marriage. You're a trooper and a much better woman than me. I think it takes a lot of courage to do what you're doing. Uh-oh, I think I'm gonna hurl," Audra said, putting her hands over her mouth. "Don't worry," she said, removing her hands. "False alarm." She laughed at herself and patted Cashmere on the hand.

Before Cashmere could reply to Audra, she was yanked up out of her chair and passed from one gorgeous hunk to the other. After twenty minutes of that, Cashmere fell, exhausted, into a chair, where she stayed until her sorority sister Tammy announced that the party was over for the bride-to-be. The announcement couldn't have come soon enough. Cashmere's energy had ebbed to an all-time low, and she was anxious for the comforts of her bed.

She said her good-byes to everyone and had no sooner exited the room when Audra was on her heels. Appearing more sober than before, Audra looked at Cashmere with an expression that Cashmere interpreted as equal parts fear and admiration. Seriously, what was up with this woman? Maybe having her fill in for Annette wasn't such a good idea after all.

"We didn't finish our conversation," Audra said.

"What conversation?" Cashmere asked, puzzled.

Audra pulled Cashmere away from the door and off to the side where they could talk privately. "I meant what I said about you being a much better woman than me, Cashmere. Honestly, I don't think I could marry a man knowing he was HIV positive. But I'm glad that your test came back negative."

Cashmere stumbled in her four-inch heels, although she had been standing still. Audra reached out a hand to steady her. "Are you okay?" she asked.

Ignoring her, Cashmere hissed, "What are you talking about?" Without waiting for the answer, she plowed on. "I know what you're up to. I peeped your game a long time ago. I asked Ray about you and him and he lied and said that you were just friends, but I know better than that—"

"Hold on!" Audra said, cutting Cashmere short. "You've got it all wrong. Raymond and I have never been anything but friends," she protested. "For one thing, I'm a married woman and I don't cheat on my husband. Secondly, I wouldn't knowingly date a man who sleeps with men." She took a deep breath and let out a sigh. "I can see that I've upset you, and for that, I apologize. I had no idea that you didn't know. Raymond told me that he had explained everything to you and that you were okay with it."

Cashmere's head was spinning. What was happening to her world? In two short weeks, she had gone from feeling like one of the luckiest people in the world to wanting to hurl herself off the Xerox Tower. Cashmere's eyes narrowed to slits. "Okay with what?" she spat.

Audra took a step back and turned as if to leave. "Look, I've said too much already . I think you need to ask Raymond."

Before Cashmere knew what was happening, she had grabbed Audra by the arm and spun her around to face her. "Hey! You're not going to come up in here the night before my wedding, drop a bomb like that on me, and not explain yourself."

Looking both startled and perplexed, Audra loosened Cashmere's grip on her arm and surveyed the crowd. Her green eyes darted from one end of the room to the other, apparently checking for on-comers. She spotted the head of Cashmere's sorority sister, Lisa, whose abnormally tall height for a woman caused her to stick out like a sore thumb in a room of women who were mostly of average height, as she approached, wearing an unpleasant expression.

"I've been looking all over for you, girl," Lisa said, approaching Cashmere. "It's getting late and you know you need at least eight hours of sleep so you won't have bags under your eyes tomorrow." Eyeing Cashmere's deer-in-the-headlights expression, Lisa asked suspiciously, "Is everything okay over here?"

"Everything's good," Cashmere lied. "Audra was just telling me some bad news about a mutual acquaintance."

Audra gave Lisa a faint smile, which seemed to satisfy the woman.

"Give me another twenty minutes and I'll be ready to go," Cashmere said dismissively.

When the two women were alone again, Audra gestured with her chin to the exit sign ten feet from where they stood and suggested they go outside to talk. The slight chill in the air raised goose bumps on the women's arms, and they rubbed vigorously to warm themselves.

Audra looked apologetically at Cashmere before speaking and cleared her throat. "Let me first say that I feel uncomfortable telling you what I'm about to. But since I was the one to unknowingly open this can of worms, I'll tell you what I know."

As Cashmere listened to Audra give her a blow-by-blow account of Raymond and Jerrold's life together, one thing became glaringly obvious to her: she didn't know Raymond at all, and she didn't know who this Jerrold person was. Raymond had told her that he had been involved with someone named Robert, she told Audra.

"Robert is Jerrold's middle name," Audra said. She continued telling Cashmere what she knew of Raymond's hidden life. When he was twenty years old, Raymond had admitted to himself that he was attracted to both sexes. Only a handful of people knew about it: Audra, Jerrold, and the other men with whom he had slept. Three years ago, Jerrold had tested positive for HIV, which was why Raymond broke off the relationship; it was obvious that Jerrold had cheated on Raymond. Cashmere had seen Raymond's test results from around that time, so she knew that Raymond was clean, or so she had thought. What she didn't know was how Raymond could go from negative to positive if she was the only one he had been with since his breakup.

"Seven months ago, right around when you two got engaged, we were on a business trip in Seattle, and Raymond contacted Jerrold because he wanted to see their adoptive daughter, Misha. One thing led to another, and they ended up spending the night together. I was very upset with him for doing that to you, but he insisted that they had used protection."

Shock was evident on Cashmere's face. Her discombobulated mind could only process one truth at a time. Involuntarily, she flashed back to the photograph she'd found in Raymond's desk. Had she been all wrong about the photograph? It was Raymond and Jerrold who had adopted a daughter, not Audra and her husband? Cashmere was having a hard time wrapping her mind around that reality. He had never told her any of this. *Why hadn't he come clean the other night while he was confessing?* "I saw a picture with you and a man and a little girl in it. Do you and your husband have children?" the question came out in a hoarse whisper.

Puzzled, Audra replied "A photogr—? Oh . . ." she said, realization dawning. "That was Jerrold and Misha in the picture. That was taken the day Raymond left Washington to move here. We were saying our good-byes at the airport."

"So wait a minute," Cashmere said, shaking her head, trying to make sense of what Audra was telling her. "Raymond and this man Jerrold adopted a daughter and Raymond walked out on his daughter?"

"No, no." Audra paused. "I'm sorry, I should have explained that." She let out a gust of air. "Misha is really Jerrold's half-sister's child. Five years ago, when she was diagnosed with stage 4 ovarian cancer and knew that she didn't have long to live, Laurel—that's Jerrold's sister's name—made arrangements to give custody of Misha to Jerrold. The father was out of the picture; in fact, he doesn't even know Misha exists, and Laurel didn't want their mother and her new husband to raise her daughter. When Raymond and Jerrold started going out, Raymond fell in love with that little girl; he's crazy about her. When their relationship looked like it was heading toward permanence, Raymond 'unofficially' adopted Misha."

Cashmere leveled a look of confusion at Audra. "What does that mean? He 'unofficially' adopted her?"

"What it means is he's really her Godfather. If anything happens to Jerrold, Raymond get's custody of Misha. At least he would have if he and Jerrold had stayed together. I believe that was something that they discussed the last time we were in Washington."

Cashmere was speechless.

Seeing Cashmere's discomfort and confusion, Audra stepped into Cashmere's space and placed a hand on her shoulder. "I know this is a lot to put on you the night before your wedding. And I know that it shows Raymond in an unflattering light. But honestly, Cashmere, Raymond loves you; I'm one hundred percent sure of that. The other day when he told me about his test, he was devastated out of his mind. He didn't know what to do. I told him to put it all out there and that if you loved him, truly loved him, then he'd know that by your reaction. When he told me that you'd come back and the wedding was still on, I assumed you knew everything. He'd even told me that you had gotten tested."

"Well, obviously, that was a lie." Her shoes were beginning to pinch her toes, but she ignored the pain; the pain was the only evidence she had that she was wide-awake and this was really happening. Out of nowhere, the statement that Raymond had made to the caller on the phone the other night skittered across her mind. With some trepidation, Cashmere asked, "When did he get tested?"

Audra appeared to think for a moment. "Almost three weeks ago," she said. "He got the results back a few days ago. Well, actually, the insurance company got the results back. He wanted to increase his life insurance policy, but he couldn't do that unless he submitted to an HIV test. The insurance company didn't deny the increase, but they said he'd have to pay some ridiculous amount in premiums for the new policy. And that's all I know."

A torrent of rage ran through her as she digested Audra's words. For all Cashmere knew, she could be infected too. She was too young to be handed such a death sentence, she thought. Although she knew the difference between HIV and AIDS, it was all the same to Cashmere; both spelled death. Cashmere's heart seemed to turn to stone within her, and a block of fear cut off the air supply to her lungs. She couldn't breathe. She couldn't think. She was having a panic attack.

Audra must have alerted Lisa, because the next thing Cashmere remembered was Lisa pulling her from the car and saying, "It's a good thing Raymond isn't home," as she ushered her into the house.

When Cashmere awoke the next morning, the only thing on her mind was revenge.

***

Her wedding gown was gorgeous: white satin and lace, with a square neckline. The sheer sleeves were inlaid with Victorian lace, and the scalloped hem pulled a cathedral train. Her round face was partly secluded behind a veil that was trimmed in the same Victorian lace as her sleeves. Her specially made satin shoes had three-and-a-half-inch heels and genuine saltwater pearl clips that ran across the tops of the shoes. She was the epitome of the beautiful bride.

As she glided down the aisle, she carried a bridal bouquet made up of an assortment of fresh flowers: lisianthus, lilies, freesia, gossamer greens, and baby's breath. The cousins leading the way, five-year-old Sadie and six-year-old Bobby, sprinkled scented potpourri on the white cloth runner. The lone child trailing behind, four-year-old Ari, carried her train.

The groom, wearing a black tailcoat, white shirt, and black cummerbund, smiled down at her. At five-foot-two and five-foot-seven, respectively, they complemented each other physically.

Cashmere's father beamed when she stopped in front of him and extended her arm. Together, father and daughter, they completed the walk.

To Raymond, he presented her, his only child.

The bride and groom faced each other. He radiated confidence, indebted to her for agreeing to be his wife.

The minister said the words he had rehearsed with them, and after securing an "I do" from Raymond, he turned to Cashmere. "Cashmere Anise Masters, do you take Raymond Alvin Lesure to be your lawfully wedded husband?"

The guests waited, their faces aglow with smiles. Her husband-to-be caressed her with his eyes.

Cashmere looked over at the handsome man named Jerrold, whom Raymond had said was a cousin, when they had made the invite list and seating chart. Raymond didn't know that Cashmere now knew who the man really was. *What a waste*, she thought. Then she looked at the happily anxious faces of the guests, then back to Raymond's smiling face. He looked so happy; her heart skipped cheerily.

When finally she answered the reverend's question, her voice was strong, loud, and clear. "No, Reverend, I do not! Raymond could never be happy with me. He's a homosexual, and he has AIDS."

BOOK CLUB DISCUSSION QUESTIONS

1.   What is unique about the different settings in the book and did those settings enhance or take away from each storyline?

2.   Was there any one particular theme that the author emphasized throughout the book or several, and what do you think it/they were? Consider each story individually.

3.   What message, if any, do you think the author was trying to get across in each story? Consider each story individually and break down its message, if there is one.

4.   Do the characters come across as real and believable?

5.   How plausible were each of the situations the characters dealt with?

6.   Can you relate to what any of the characters went through?

7.   Do any of the characters remind you of yourself or anyone you know?

8.   Consider each story individually. How do the characters evolve or change in each story? Is there any specific event that triggers the change?

9.   Do you think the stories reveal the author's world view? In what ways?

10. Did any of the events in the storylines make you feel uncomfortable? If so, in what way? Did it make you more self aware, or lead to a different understanding of an aspect of your life that you hadn't previously held?

11. If you could re-write any one scene in the book, which one would it be and why?

ABOUT THE AUTHOR

Cathy Jo has been writing since the age of eleven. She lives in a little house in a suburb of Cleveland, Ohio with her dust bunnies. She is a graduate of the Cleveland Public School system.

Among Cathy Jo's most cherished childhood memories are frequent visits to the old Treasure House library on Crawford Road, where her mother encouraged her to spend time reading. In 1980 when she was hired as a Page at the Cleveland Public library, her love for reading and writing was further fostered when she began working in the Literature department, where she discovered such authors as Daphne du Maurier, Jane Austen, Toni Morrison, Erma Bombeck, and Nikki Giovanni.

Cathy Jo began writing her collection of short stories over 10 years ago, after she completed her first novel. Three of the stories in the collection are from that novel. Currently, she is working on completing a second collection of short stories and a second novel. Not necessarily in that order.